"We make a good team, you and me."

"You're drunk, Evan."

"Maybe a little."

"Your judgment is impaired."

"My judgment is perfect. You're incredible, Angie. And I wanted you just as badly sober as I do now."

Before she realized what was happening, his lips were on hers. Magic exploded inside her brain, colors flashing, music playing, the taste of Evan overwhelming her senses. The kiss went on for long minutes before he finally pulled back.

She was breathless, and not nearly as horrified as she ought to have been. She had to get it together here.

"That did not demonstrate good judgment, Evan," she told him tartly, holding out her hand for the car keys.

He just grinned and dropped the keys into her palm. "Sure it did."

* * *

Reunited with th…
Dynasti…
A Wyoming lege…

If yo…
tell us what you t… Harlequin Desire!
#harlequindesire

Dear Reader,

I was delighted to be included in Harlequin Desire's Dynasties: The Lassiters continuity series. It's always exciting to collaborate with so many other talented authors, and writing the final story in a series is enormously satisfying.

In *Reunited with the Lassiter Bride,* Angelica Lassiter is thrown together with her ex-fiancé, Evan McCain, and forced to come to terms with her lingering feelings for him. I love a reunion romance, especially one where the breakup is recent and emotions are intense. The stakes for Lassiter Media are high, but the stakes for Angelica and Evan are even higher as they navigate through guilt, mistrust and apparent betrayal to rediscover their love.

I hope you enjoy *Reunited with the Lassiter Bride.*

Happy reading!

Barbara

REUNITED WITH THE
LASSITER BRIDE

—

BARBARA DUNLOP

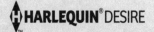

Special thanks and acknowledgment are given to Barbara Dunlop for her contribution to the Dynasties: The Lassiters miniseries.

Recycling programs
for this product may
not exist in your area.

ISBN-13: 978-0-373-73337-8

REUNITED WITH THE LASSITER BRIDE

Printed in U.S.A.

www.Harlequin.com

Books by Barbara Dunlop

Harlequin Desire

Silhouette Desire

*Montana Millionaires: The Ryders
^Colorado Cattle Barons

Other titles by this author available in ebook format.

BARBARA DUNLOP

writes romantic stories while curled up in a log cabin in Canada's far north, where bears outnumber people and it snows six months of the year. Fortunately she has a brawny husband and two teenage children to haul firewood and clear the driveway while she sips cocoa and muses about her upcoming chapters. Barbara loves to hear from readers. You can contact her through her website, www.barbaradunlop.com.

For my sisters, with love.

One

There were days when Evan McCain wished he'd never met the Lassiter family. Today was definitely one of them. Thanks to J. D. Lassiter, at thirty-four years old, Evan was starting his professional life all over again.

He pushed open the door to his empty storefront office building in Santa Monica. By rights, he should have sold the compact building two years ago after moving to Pasadena, but it was only a block from the beach and the investment value was solid. As things turned out, he was very glad he'd kept it.

He had no intention of touching any of the money left to him by J.D. The bequest in his former boss's will felt like a payoff for Evan's unwitting participation in J.D.'s complex scheme to test his daughter Angelica, Evan's ex-fiancée. She'd eventually passed the test, proving she could balance her work and her life, and replaced Evan at the helm of Lassiter Media. But she'd failed Evan in the process, ending both their romantic relationship and his employment at Lassiter Media.

He dropped his suitcase in the reception area, hit the overhead lights and moved to the counter to test the telephone. He got a dial tone and mentally checked off two steps in his implementation plan. He had electricity, and he was connected to the outside world. Those were the basics.

The blinds on the glass door rattled as someone opened it behind him.

"Oh, how the mighty have fallen." It was the voice of his long-time friend Deke Leamon.

Evan turned, blinking against the streaming sunlight, baffled to see Deke silhouetted in his doorway. "What on earth are you doing on the West Coast?"

Deke grinned, dropping a red duffel bag on the vinyl reception seat beside Evan's suitcase. He was dressed in faded jeans, a Mets T-shirt, and a pair of scruffy hikers. "We did it before. We can do it again."

Evan stepped forward to shake his former college roommate's hand. "Do what again? Seriously, why didn't you call? And how did you know I'd be here?"

"Educated guess," said Deke. "I figured there'd be too many memories in Pasadena. This seemed like the logical place. I assume you're going to live upstairs for a while?"

"Good guess," said Evan.

The upstairs apartment was small, but he'd make it work. He needed an immediate and total change of scenery. Luckily, despite its proximity to downtown L.A., Santa Monica had a personality all its own.

"Figured you might be feeling sorry for yourself," Deke continued. "So, I thought I'd wander over and give you a kick in the ass."

"I'm not feeling sorry for myself," said Evan.

Life was what it was, and no amount of complaining or wishing would change it to something else. It was a hard lesson, but he'd learned long ago that he could roll with the punches. On his seventeenth birthday to be exact, he'd realized just how resilient he could be.

"And you don't wander," he finished.

His friend was contemplative and deliberate in every action he undertook. Deke didn't do anything on a whim. Now, he dropped into one of the vinyl chairs and stretched out his legs, crossing them at the ankles.

"Okay, so I flew here on purpose." He glanced around the empty office space. "Thought I could probably lend a hand."

Evan leaned back against the reception countertop, bracing himself and raising a challenging brow. "Lend a hand doing what, exactly?"

"Whatever needs doin'." Deke glanced around the office. "So, what's the plan? What happens first?"

"The phones are up and running." Evan realized that he was still holding the cordless receiver, and he set it down.

"Good start. You got any leads? Got a website?"

Evan was both touched and amused by what he knew Deke was doing. "You don't need to be here."

"I want to be here. I left Colby in charge at Tiger Tech. Told him I'd be back in a month or so."

Colby Payne was a young, innovative genius who'd been Deke's second in command for two years.

"That's ridiculous." Evan wasn't about to let Deke make that kind of sacrifice. "I don't need your pity. Even if I wanted you here—which I don't—you've got a business to run."

Deke's massive technological prototyping facility in Chicago was filled with everything from computerized lathes to 3D printers. It helped budding innovators turn their ideas into commercial products. His unique brand of savvy and entrepreneurship had launched dozens of success ventures.

Deke shrugged. "I was getting bored. I haven't taken a vacation in two years."

"Go to Paris or Hawaii."

Deke grinned. "I'd go stir-crazy in Hawaii."

"You've seen the tourism photos, right? The surf, the sand, the girls in bikinis?"

"There are girls in bikinis right here in Santa Monica."

"I can take care of myself, Deke."

Sure, it was a blow, summarily losing his job with Lassiter Media when J.D.'s will codicil kicked in and gave control of the company to Evan's ex-fiancée Angelica. But he was already on the road to recovery.

"Don't you remember how much fun we had?" Deke asked. "You, me, Lex, holed up in that crappy apartment in Venice Beach, worrying about student debt while we tried to build a business?"

"It was fun when we were twenty-three."

"It'll be fun again."

"We failed," Evan noted.

Instead of getting rich, the three of them ended up going their separate ways. Deke went into technology, Evan into business management, while Lex Baldwin was rising fast in the ranks of Asanti International, a luxury hotel chain.

"Yeah, but we're way smarter now."

Evan couldn't stop a chopped laugh. "All evidence to the contrary?"

"Okay, I'm smarter now."

"I want to be completely on my own this time," said Evan.

He'd enjoyed working with J. D. Lassiter. The man was a genius. But he'd also turned out to be a manipulative old schemer. Family came first for J.D., always. And since Evan wasn't family, he'd ended up as collateral damage when J.D. had set out to test the loyalty of his daughter.

Not that Evan blamed anyone for supporting their own family. If he'd had a family, he'd have supported them through thick and thin. But he had no brothers or sisters. And his parents had died in a car accident the day he turned seventeen.

He'd planned to have children with Angelica. He wanted a big family, big enough that none of them would ever have to be alone. But that obviously wasn't going to happen now.

"I've got your back," Deke told him, his tone low and sincere as he scrutinized Evan's expression.

"I don't need anybody to have my back."

"Everybody needs somebody."

"I thought I had Angie." As soon as the words were out, Evan regretted them.

"But you didn't."

"I know."

Angie had seemed like the woman of Evan's dreams. But she'd bolted at the first sign of trouble. She'd turned her back on him and everybody else, isolating herself, refusing to trust him or her family.

"Better you found out before the wedding."

"Sure," Evan agreed, because it was the easiest thing to do.

Secretly, he couldn't help but wonder what might have happened if J.D. had passed away after the wedding. As his wife, would Angie have tried any harder to trust him?

"She's out of your life, Evan."

"I know that."

"You don't look like a man who knows that."

"I've got my head on straight. It's over. I get that. I'm here in Santa Monica because it's over."

Maybe Evan would find someone else someday. Not that he could imagine when, how or who. If Angie wasn't the real thing, he couldn't fathom who was.

"I'm going to hold you to that," said Deke, coming to his feet, rubbing his hands together. "Okay, first up, we get your business back on its feet. At the very least, your accomplishments at Lassiter Media will impress future clients."

"They will be impressed," Evan agreed. They'd be impressed with what he'd accomplished there. Some might even be impressed that he'd walked away.

* * *

Angelica Lassiter needed a fresh start. If there was a Reset button for life, she'd press it right now.

She'd fought with her family over her father's will for five long months, only to discover J.D. had a master plan all along to test her ability to balance work with life. Although he'd first seemed to hand it to Evan, in the end, her father had given her exactly what she longed for: control of Lassiter Media. But she wasn't proud of the way she'd fought for it. And she wasn't proud of the way she'd treated Evan.

It was bad enough that she'd pushed her ex-fiancé away while she fought for her heritage. But she'd accused him of lying to her, of betraying her and conspiring to steal her inheritance. She'd been wrong on all counts, but there was no way to take it back.

"Ms. Lassiter?" Her administrative assistant appeared in the doorway of the empty boardroom.

"Yes, Becky." Angelica turned from where she was gazing across the heart of downtown L.A.

"The decorators are here."

Angelica squared her shoulders and gave her assistant a determined nod. "Thanks, Becky. Please show them in."

Angelica knew her decision to renovate the top floor of the Lassiter building and relocate the CEO's office was going to cause a lot of talk within the company. But she also knew it was her only option.

Maybe if the power transition had gone smoothly she could have moved directly into her father's office. After all, she'd been at the helm in all but title prior to her father's death. But with the original will leaving control to Evan, the transition had been anything but smooth. And now she needed to put her own stamp on Lassiter Media. She'd decided to convert the top floor boardroom into her own office and turn her father's office into a boardroom.

"Angelica." Suzanne Smith entered the room first, followed by her partner Boswell Cruz. "It's so good to see you again."

Suzanne's expression and tone were professional, but she couldn't quite hide the curiosity lurking in her eyes. The Lassiter family's troubles had been all over the media these past months. Angelica couldn't really blame Suzanne for wondering what would happen next.

"Thanks for coming on such short notice," said Angelica, moving forward to shake both of their hands. "Hello, Boswell."

"Nice to see you again, Angelica," he returned.

"Tell me how we can help you," said Suzanne. Her expression invited confidence.

"I'd like to build new office. For me. Right here."

Suzanne waited for a moment, but Angelica didn't offer anything more.

"Okay," said Suzanne, gazing around at the polished beech wood paneling and the picture windows on two sides of the room. "I have always loved this space."

"It'll give me some extra light in the morning," said Angelica, repeating the rationale she'd decided to use for the move.

"Light is good."

"And J.D.'s old office is closer to the floor's reception area, so it'll make a more convenient boardroom." It was another perfectly plausible excuse that had nothing to do with Angelica's real reasons for making the switch.

Boswell had a tablet in his hand and was already making notes.

"Anything in particular you want to keep from J.D.'s office?" asked Suzanne. "Furniture pieces? Art?"

"Nothing," said Angelica.

The twitch of Suzanne's mouth betrayed her surprise at the answer.

"Maybe keep the historic Big Blue mural," Angelica

added, rethinking the sweeping decision. "It can hang in the new boardroom."

The painting of the Lassiter ranch in Wyoming had hung in J.D.'s office for over a decade. Moving it would cause talk and speculation, possibly even more speculation than Angelica's moving her office to the opposite end of the thirtieth floor.

She wasn't turning her back on her roots. And, despite what the tabloids had surmised, she had forgiven her father. Or at least she would forgive her father, eventually, though maybe not all at once. Emotionally, she had to sort some things through first.

"That's it?" asked Suzanne. Her tone was neutral, but it didn't quite mask her surprise. Some of J.D.'s pieces were very valuable antiques.

"We can put the rest in storage."

"Certainly. Did you have any initial thoughts on your office?"

"Lots of natural light," said Angelica. "I like the fresh feel of the atrium, so plants for sure. Not ultra-modern, no chrome or anything. And I don't want bright white. But definitely lighter tones, neutrals, earth tones perhaps." She paused. "Am I making any sense?"

"This is all good," Suzanne assured her. "It gives us a nice starting point. Now, you've got plenty of room in here. You'll want a desk area, a meeting table, and a lounge area. Would you like us to include a wet bar? A private washroom?"

"Only if you can do it discreetly. I want it to look like a business office, not a playboy's downtown loft."

Suzanne's alarm showed on her face. "Oh, no. It won't look anything like that."

"It would be nice to be able to offer refreshments."

"Done," said Suzanne. "And we'll make it discreet, I promise."

The door opened and Becky appeared again. "Ms. Lassiter? Sorry to interrupt. But your three o'clock is here."

"We'll get out of your way," said Suzanne. "Would the end of the week be soon enough for some mock-ups?"

"End of the week is fine," said Angelica.

She'd rather have the mock-ups in the next ten minutes, but patience was one of the characteristics she was practicing at the moment. Patience, composure and a work-life balance.

Before his sudden death, her father had complained that she worked too hard, that she needed balance in her life. When he'd taken away her position at Lassiter through his will, she'd been forced to reevaluate her balance.

She'd made progress, and she'd promised herself to give it a fair shot. She was even thinking about taking up a hobby, and maybe a sport. Yoga, perhaps. People who did yoga seemed very serene.

"We'll be in touch," said Suzanne as she and Boswell left the boardroom.

The door closed behind them, and Angelica took a moment to focus on her composure. Her next meeting was with her close friend Kayla Prince. Kayla was engaged to Lassiter Media account executive Matt Hollis, so she'd been along for the ride on the family discord over the past five months.

Angelica knew that many of the Lassiter Media executives worried she'd put the company at risk by working with corporate raider Jack Reed and attempting to contest the will. And her recent single-minded focus on regaining control of the company meant she hadn't seen much of Kayla or any of her other friends. She could only imagine what Kayla might have heard from Matt at the height of the conflict.

So, when the door opened again, she was ready for anything. But Kayla surprised her, rushing through the door and quickly pulling her into a warm hug.

"I'm so glad it's over," said Kayla. She drew back to peer

at Angelica. "You okay now? Congratulations. You deserved this all along. You're going to be a fantastic CEO."

Angelica's brain stumbled for a moment, and then a warm rush of relief nearly buckled her knees. She hugged Kayla back. "I've missed you so much," she confessed.

"Whose fault is that?" Kayla asked on a laugh.

"Mine. It's all my fault. Everything is all my fault."

Kayla drew back again, this time briskly rubbing Angelica's upper arms. "Stop. That's enough. I don't want to hear you say that again."

Angelica was about to protest, but then she spotted Tiffany Baines in the doorway. "Tiff?"

Tiffany opened her arms, and Angelica rushed to greet her other close friend.

"Angie," Tiffany sighed. "It's so great to see you at the office."

Angelica took a step back, sobering. "I've got a lot of work to do here." She glanced at Kayla as well. "There are a lot of fences to mend and a whole lot of decisions to make."

"You'll do great," Tiffany stated with conviction. "There's nobody better than you to run Lassiter Media. The stupid will put you in an impossible position."

"I could have handled it better," said Angelica.

"How were you to know it was a test? What if it hadn't been a test? What if your father had truly lost his mind and left the family company to Evan? You were right to fight it."

"I think you're the only person in the world who feels that way," Angelica said to Tiffany.

"I doubt it. But it doesn't matter. What matters now is that you're going to be an amazing success." A mischievous grin grew on Tiffany's face, and she shifted her attention to Kayla. "Go ahead. Tell her."

"Tell me what?" Angelica took in Kayla's matching, wide grin. "What's going on?"

"We've set a date," said Kayla.

"For the wedding?"

Kayla nodded.

"That's fantastic news. When? Where? How big?"

Kayla laughed. "End of September. I know it's quick. But they had a cancellation at the Emerald Wave. We'll be oceanfront in Malibu, just like my mother always dreamed we'd be. We can have the ceremony right on the cliff. I know it'll be spectacular."

"It sounds perfect," said Angelica, ignoring the tiny spear of jealousy that tried to pierce her chest.

It was too late for her own fairy-tale wedding. That was simply the reality of it all. And she was genuinely delighted for her friend.

"Now that we've finally made plans, I can't wait to marry Matt."

"Of course you can't."

"I want you to be my maid of honor."

The jealousy was immediately obliterated by a wave of warmth. Angelica was surprised and touched. "I'd love to be your maid of honor. After everything—" she stopped, gathering her emotions. "You are so sweet to ask."

"Sweet, nothing. You're my best friend. You always have been, and you always will be."

"And I'm going to be a bridesmaid," sang Tiffany. "We're going to have a blast."

"We are," Angelica agreed, putting conviction into her tone. "This is exactly what I need right now."

She *would* forgive her father. And she truly did want to honor his wishes. What could be more conducive to work-life balance than being maid of honor at a wedding?

Kayla's expression tightened ever so slightly. "There is one small complication."

"What's that?"

"Matt is going to ask Evan to be the best man."

Angelica's equilibrium faltered.

Evan as the best man, while she was the maid of honor? She and Evan together, dressed to the nines, at a dream wedding with lace, flowers and champagne, but not getting married? For a second, she didn't think she could do it. She didn't see how she could survive an event like that.

"Angelica?" Kayla prompted, worry in her tone.

"It's fine," said Angelica, her voice only slightly high-pitched. "It'll be fine." She gave a little laugh through her fear. "Hey, unless he leaves L.A., we're going to run into each other eventually. I can handle it. No problem." She gained determination. "I'm going to be the best maid of honor ever."

Angelica's sanctuary was the rose garden at her family's mansion in Beverly Hills. She'd had the gazebo built five years ago to take advantage of the quiet, fragrant setting. At the end of a busy day, filled with dozens of meetings and the blare of the television screens that followed the five Lassiter networks, she could settle into one of the padded Adirondack chairs and sip a glass of wine.

It was peaceful out here. She could read through the latest ratings, check reviews on the programming from Lassiter Broadcast System, take note of the successes and failures of the competition, and wrap her head around strategic directions for each of the Lassiter Media networks. It might only be September, but contingency plans for the inevitable January scheduling adjustments were well underway.

She heard footfalls on the brick pathway from the main house and assumed it would be a member of the kitchen staff checking to see if she wanted dinner. She really wasn't hungry, and she didn't want to give up the peace of the garden just yet. She'd ask them to hold it for her.

"Hello, Angelica," came a distinct, male voice that sent a buzz of reaction twisting down her spine. She tightened the grip on her wine glass, whirling her head to see if she was imagining him.

She wasn't. Evan was standing in the middle of her rose garden, his steel-gray shirt open at the collar, and a pair of faded blue jeans clinging to his hips. His unshaven jaw was set, his hazel eyes dark and guarded.

"Evan?" she responded, memories of the times they spent out here coming to life in her mind. They'd made love more than once in this gazebo, the cool, evening breeze kissing their sweaty skin, the scent of roses wafting over them, the taste of red wine on his lips.

She swiftly set down her wineglass.

He took a couple of steps forward, coming to a halt at the short staircase that led up to the gazebo. "I hope you're ready to put on your maid-of-honor hat."

She sat up straighter, taking in his expression. "Why? Does Kayla need something? Is something wrong?"

"Yes, something's wrong." He paused. "I'd never show up here unless something was very wrong."

The disdainful words cut her to the core. He didn't want to be at the mansion, didn't want anything more to do with her. She understood that. She'd prefer to stay away from him as well, but not for the same reasons.

They'd been forced into each other's company on several occasions since the breakup. Through it all, she'd had her anger to shield her. But now, all that was left was embarrassment and guilt.

"You heard Matt and Kayla were delayed in Scotland?" he asked.

She told herself to brazen it out. Evan couldn't read her mind.

"Yes," she said. "Matt called in to the office yesterday. He's taking a few extra days of vacation."

Matt and Kayla had flown to Edinburgh to take advantage of a last-minute opportunity to secure a significant art exhibit for Kayla's gallery. As Angelica understood it, after they'd arrived, they'd been told a senior member of the church council had to personally approve some of the pieces leaving the country. They'd been forced to travel to his retreat in the north of the country to meet with him.

"I've been trying to call them all day," Evan continued. "But with the time difference and the spotty cell reception in the countryside, I couldn't get through. And then I thought to myself, what are they going to do from Scotland anyway except worry? We'll have to fix it for them from here."

"Fix what?" She sat up straighter. "What's wrong, Evan?"

He put his foot on the first stair and braced his hand on a support post, but seemed unwilling to enter the gazebo. "There was a fire at the Emerald Wave."

"Oh, no. Was it bad?"

"Bad enough. It gutted half the kitchen. Luckily, nobody was hurt."

Angelica was grateful to hear everyone was safe, but her mind immediately went to Kayla. "We're only three weeks from the wedding."

"No kidding."

"We need to find them a new venue."

"Are you going to continue stating the obvious?"

She felt her nerves snap to attention. "Are you going to continue being a jerk?"

"Oh, Angie." His tone was soft, and his use of her nickname sent a new shiver of awareness through her body. "I haven't even begun being a jerk."

She reached for her glass of merlot, needing something to fortify her. "What do you want from me, Evan?"

He came up the three steps, filling the doorway to the gazebo with his six-foot-two height. "I need your help. I went to see Conrad Norville today."

"I don't understand." What did movie mogul Conrad Norville have to do with repairing a kitchen?

"To ask if we could use his Malibu mansion for the wedding."

The explanation set her back for a moment. But she had to admit, it was a good idea.

Conrad Norville owned a monster of a mansion on the Malibu oceanfront. The seventy-something man was renowned for being gruff and eccentric, but his house was acknowledged as an architectural masterpiece.

"It's the only place anywhere near Malibu that has a hope of fitting all the guests," said Evan.

"What did he say?"

"He told me, and I'm quoting here, 'No way in hell am I getting mixed up with that Lassiter circus. I've got a reputation to protect.'"

Angelica felt her defenses go up on behalf of her family. "*He's* got a reputation to protect?"

"No," said Evan, his tone admonishing. "He's got a house we want to borrow."

"But—"

"Don't get all high and mighty—"

"I'm *not* high and mighty."

"Well, whatever you are, this is no time for you to get into a fight with the man."

"He already turned you down," Angelica pointed out. How could it possibly matter if she fought with Norville or not?

"I'm willing to take another run at it," said Evan. "For Matt and Kayla's sake."

The statement made her curious. "You think you can change his mind?"

"I was thinking *you* could help me change his mind."

"How could I do that? I've barely met him in passing. And it sure doesn't sound as though he likes my family."

"I thought we could alleviate his fears, present a united front. Show him there are no hard feelings between us, that the rumors about the power struggle were overblown."

The rumors weren't overblown. When her father's will left

control of Lassiter Media to Evan, it had resulted in all-out battle between the two of them. Even now, when they both knew it had been a test of her loyalty, their spirits were battered and bruised, their relationship shattered beyond repair.

But Kayla's happiness was at stake. Or, more specifically, Kayla's mother's happiness was at stake. Angelica was willing to bet that Kayla would marry Matt anywhere. In fact, they'd probably prefer to be married in Cheyenne, where they'd made their home. But Kayla's mother had been looking forward to this day since Kayla was born. And Kayla would do anything for her family.

"So, you're asking me to lie?" Angelica stated in a flat, uncompromising tone.

"I'm asking you to lie," Evan agreed.

"For Kayla and Matt." That might be one of the few reasons she'd consider it.

"I'd do a lot more than lie for Matt," said Evan.

She took in the determination on his handsome face. Experience had taught her that he was a formidable opponent who let absolutely nothing stand in his way.

"I shudder to think how far you'd go to get what you want."

His expression tightened. "Yeah? Well, we both know how far you'll go, don't we?"

It was a cutting blow.

"I thought I was protecting my family," she defended.

When she'd learned of the terms of the will, she couldn't come up with any explanation except that her father had lost his mind, or that Evan had brazenly manipulated J.D. into leaving him control of Lassiter Media.

"You figured you were right and everyone else was wrong?" he asked.

"It seemed so at the time."

His steps toward her appeared automatic. "You slept in

my arms, told me you loved me, and then accused me of defrauding you out of nearly a billion dollars."

All the pieces had added up in her mind back then, and they had been damning for Evan. "Seducing me would have been an essential part of your overall plan to steal Lassiter Media."

"Shows you how little you know about me."

"I guess it does."

Even though she was agreeing, the answer seemed to anger him.

"You *should* have known me. You should have trusted me. My nefarious plan was all inside your suspicious little head. I never made it, never mind executed it."

"I had no way of knowing that at the time."

"You could have trusted me. That's what wives do with their husbands."

"We never got married."

"Your decision, not mine."

They stared at each other for a long moment.

"What do you want me to do?" she finally asked. Then she realized her question was ambiguous. "About Conrad."

An ironic half smile played on Evan's lips. "Don't worry. I know you'd never ask what I wanted you to do about us."

He backed off a couple of paces. "Come with me to see Conrad. Tomorrow night. Pretend we're pals, that everything is terrific between us, and he doesn't have to worry about any public fights."

The request brought a pain to Angelica's stomach. Nothing was remotely terrific between her and Evan. He was angry and she was sad. Because now that their dispute over Lassiter Media was over, she missed so many things about their former life.

"Sure," she agreed, forcing her misery into a small corner of her soul. "I'll do whatever it takes to help Kayla."

"I'll pick you up at seven. Wear something feminine."

She glanced down at her slim, navy skirt and the collared, white blouse. "Feminine?"

"You know, ruffles or flowers, and some pretty shoes. Maybe curl your hair."

"Curl my hair?"

"You don't want to look like my rival. He's an old-fashioned guy, Angie. He remembers a different time, a different kind of woman."

"When? The 1950s?"

"That sounds about right."

"You want me to simper and giggle and bat my eyelashes to get a wedding venue for Kayla and Matt."

"In a word, yes."

She'd do it. She'd definitely do it for her best friend. But she wasn't going to like it, and she wasn't going into it without a protest. "Shall I cling to your arm as well?"

"Cling to anything you want. Just sell it to him." With that pronouncement, Evan turned on his heel, left the gazebo and disappeared along the pathway.

Two

Evan stood in the high-ceilinged foyer of the Lassiter mansion, gazing in amazement as a transformed Angie descended the grand staircase. She looked beautiful, feminine and deceptively sweet. Her chestnut hair was half up, half down, wisps dangling at her temples and curling enticingly along her shoulders in a silk curtain. The color was lighter than he remembered it, and he instantly realized he liked it this way.

"You're wearing pink," he couldn't stop himself from observing.

"Now who's stating the obvious?" As she covered the last couple of stairs, Evan noticed her simple, white pumps that matched a tiny purse tucked under her arm.

"I've never seen you in pink." The dress was snug in the bodice, with cap sleeves and flat lace across the chest. It had a full silk skirt and a discreet ruffle along the hem. She wore simple diamond stud earrings and a tiny diamond pendant on a delicate gold chain. She truly could have stepped out of the 1950s.

"I hate pink," she noted as she came to a halt on the ground floor. Then she donned a brilliant if slightly strained smiled and pirouetted in front of him. "But do you think this outfit will get Kayla the dream Malibu wedding her mother wants for her?"

Evan wasn't sure the outfit would get them a wedding. But it was definitely getting him turned on. He'd seen Angie in no-nonsense suits, opulent evening gowns and the occasional classic black cocktail dress. But he'd never seen her looking so alluring and demure, and so incredibly kissable.

"If it doesn't," Evan found himself responding, "nothing will."

"Good." Her expression relaxed, and her smile looked more natural. "Then let's get this over with, shall we?"

He held out his arm to escort her, but she didn't take it. She walked pointedly past him, drawing open the front door and marching onto the porch.

"He needs to believe we're still friends," Evan cautioned as he trotted down the staircase after her.

His dark blue Miata convertible was parked halfway around the circular driveway. He'd picked Angie up in this spot countless times, taking her to dinners, to parties, occasionally away for the weekend. And for a few heartbeats, it felt exactly like old times. He had to stop himself from taking her hand or putting an arm around her shoulders. Touching her seemed like such a natural thing to do.

"I can act," she responded breezily.

He slipped past her to open the passenger door. "I'm sure you can."

She slid into the low seat, pulling her dainty shoes in behind her. "Conrad knows we're coming?"

"He knows. I imagine we'll get an earful about some of the stories in the tabloids."

"I can cope with upset people."

"Can you keep your cool when they come after your family?"

"Of course, I can."

"Angie?" Evan cautioned.

She stared straight ahead. "Don't call me that."

"You want me to call you Ms. Lassiter?"

"My name is Angelica."

He waited for a moment, until curiosity got the better of her and she raised her eyes to look his way.

"Not to me it isn't," he told her firmly. Then he pushed the door shut and rounded the hood of the car.

He knew he shouldn't goad her, and he probably shouldn't use her nickname either. But they'd been lovers once, best friends, engaged. They'd been mere hours away from getting married. They'd laughed. They'd fought. And she'd cried naked in his arms. He wasn't about to pretend it had all never happened.

They both stayed silent as he pulled onto Sunset, pointing the sports car toward the Pacific Coast Highway.

"You can do it for one night," she told him as he navigated traffic beneath the bright streetlights.

"Do what for one night?" He wondered if she was aware of the many interesting ways that statement could be taken.

She'd probably slap his face if she knew what he was picturing right now.

His mouth flexed in a half smile at his own thoughts. If this really were the 1950s, she would slap his face, but he'd kiss her anyway, pinning her hard against the nearest wall. Then she'd quickly capitulate and kiss him back, because she was only protesting out of a duty to be a good girl, not because she was unwilling.

"Call me Angie," she answered, startling him out of the daydream.

"I can call you Angie for one night?"

"While we're at Conrad Norville's pretending to be friends. But that's it."

"I don't think you can control what I call you," he countered casually.

She fussed with the hem of her skirt, and there was something defiant in her tone. "I can control what I call you."

"Call me anything you like."

"What about incompetent and irresponsible?"

"Excuse me?" He swung a glance her way for a second before returning his attention to the winding highway. "You're planning to insult me in front of Norville?"

"Not Norville. I had a phone call this morning. Somebody looking for a reference on your work with Lassiter Media."

"Who?" Evan immediately asked.

"Lyle Dunstand from Eden International."

Anger clenched his stomach, and his tone went iron-hard. "You'd actually undermine my business out of spite?"

She was silent for a moment. "Relax, Evan. I told them you'd done a fantastic job under trying circumstances. I gave you complete credit for last year's expansion into Britain and Australia, and I said your instincts for people were second to none."

His anger dissipated as quickly as it had formed.

"My point is," she continued. "I'm treating you with respect and professionalism. You could at least do the same for me."

"I didn't give anyone your contact information," he assured her. "I was hoping they'd avoid checking with Lassiter."

"I can't see that happening. You were with us for several years." She angled her body to face him. "So, you're opening up the consulting agency again."

"I have to earn a living."

"My father left you a lot of money."

Evan coughed out a cold laugh. "Like I'm going to touch Lassiter money."

She seemed to consider his words. "Are you angry with him?"

"Hell, yes, I'm angry with him. He used me. He messed with my life like I was some pawn in his private game."

"He assumed we'd be married by the time he died."

Evan twisted his head to look at her again. "And that makes it better? He sets me up as CEO in order to test your loyalty to him, and then he cuts me loose to do what? Play second fiddle to my own wife at Lassiter?"

She seemed to consider his statement. "Are you saying you'd have a problem working for me? If we were married, I mean?"

"Yes."

"But you'd have been okay with me working for you?"

He gave a shrug. "It might not be logical or fair. But, yeah, I could live with that."

"Now who's living in the 1950s?"

He didn't disagree. "It's a moot point. Neither of those things is ever going to happen."

"Because we'll never be married."

"Stating the obvious again, Angie."

"Angelica."

"You said I could have one night." He wheeled the car into a left turn, and down the private road that led to Conrad Norville's estate.

They met Conrad in the great room of his oceanfront residence. Even though Angelica had spent years living in the Lassiter mansion, she was taken aback by the size and opulence of the home. The great room was accessed through a massive foyer and a marble pillared hallway decorated in ivory and gold. The room was huge, rectangular, with a thirty-foot ceiling. Its beachside wall was completely made of glass. In the center of the glass wall, several panels were drawn aside, turning the patio into an extension of the house.

The patio itself was beautifully set up for entertaining, with different tiers that held tables, comfortable lounge furniture groupings, and gas fire pits surrounded by padded chairs. The lowest tier jutted out over a cliff, offering a spectacular view of the rocks and waves, while a side area held a swimming pool, complete with a pool house and a massive wet bar.

As Conrad shook her hand in welcome, he gave Angelica's outfit a critical once over. He didn't make any comment, and she couldn't tell what he thought.

"Your family's been in the news lately," he stated, giving a signal to a waiting butler who immediately moved forward with a silver tray of drinks.

"Things have stabilized now," said Angelica, standing next to the open doorways, appreciating the fresh ocean breeze. "I think we're all ready to move forward on a positive path."

"You never want to become the story." Conrad took a crystal glass from the waiter's tray. It contained a small quantity of amber liquid.

"Being in the media wasn't something any of us enjoyed," Angelica agreed.

The butler offered her a drink, and she took it, guessing it was probably single malt, since Conrad owned a distillery in Scotland and often sang its praises. She hated single malt, but she'd drink it if she had to.

"Is your daddy a crazy man?" Conrad asked, studying her expression while he waited for her answer.

Though they'd tried to guard the details of J.D.'s will, with Conrad's industry and social contacts, he'd likely have learned more than most people outside the family.

Before she could answer, Evan stepped in. "J. D. Lassiter loved his family very much. It's one of the things I admired most about him."

"My stepkids are leeches," said Conrad, switching his piercing attention to Evan. "No good, blood-sucking losers."

Angelica glanced at Evan, but he didn't seem to know how to respond to that either.

"I'm sorry to hear that," she offered into the awkward silence. "Do they live here in Malibu?"

Conrad gave a gruff laugh. "Can't afford their own houses. At least not the kind of houses they think they deserve." He upended his glass, swallowing the entire shot.

Angelica took an experimental sip. It was single malt all right—bold, peaty scotch that nearly peeled the skin from her mouth.

Evan finished his in one swallow.

"They're both in Monaco right now," said Conrad, signaling the butler to bring another round. "Some fancy car race through the city. Nothing but girls and all-night parties, I'm guessing."

"Kayla Prince runs an art gallery," Evan offered. As he spoke, he shifted a little closer to Angelica.

She assumed he was trying to perpetuate the ruse that they were still good friends.

"One of those snooty, high-brow places?" Conrad asked. "Always trying to get me to spend millions on some nouveau crap. Can't even tell what's in those pictures. A monkey might have done it for all I can tell."

"I once bought a water color painted by an elephant," said Angelica.

Her instinct was to defend Kayla, but she didn't want to risk an argument with Conrad. She decided it was better to distract him with a new thread of conversation.

Evan gave her a puzzled look, but Conrad jumped right in on the topic.

"Could you tell what it was?"

"Blue and pink lines. The elephant's name was Sunny. Cost me five hundred dollars."

That got a grin from Conrad. "The elephant's probably more talented than that artist, and he charges millions. One of the kids bid at an art auction last month, and I nearly had to mortgage my house."

She found herself glancing around while she tried to imagine how much you'd have to bid at an auction to warrant a mortgage on this particular house.

The butler returned, and while Conrad was distracted, Evan smoothly switched glasses with Angelica, discreetly downing her drink. She couldn't help finding the action chivalrous. She attempted to refuse a second drink, but Conrad insisted, so she accepted, declaring the scotch delicious.

"You probably want to see the patio," Conrad said to Angelica, sounding like he didn't particularly want to show it to her.

"I would love to see the patio."

He gestured. "Well, come on outside. Evan here says you're going to convince me the scandal is over, and it's safe to be associated with the Lassiters."

"The scandal is over," she assured him as they stepped outside.

Soft, recessed lights came on in the perimeter gardens, whether triggered by motion sensor or an alert staff member, Angelica couldn't tell.

"And you're at the helm now?" Conrad asked her.

"I am."

Conrad looked to Evan.

"She's at the helm," Evan agreed. "And she'll do a fantastic job."

Though she knew he was only playing a part, Evan's words warmed her.

Conrad got a cagey expression on his face. "Angelica, while I'm deciding whether or not to lend you my mansion, what would you say if I told you Norville Productions had a series we think would be perfect for Lassiter Broadcast System?"

"I'd tell you at LBS we have always created our own programming."

"And if I reminded you that I have something you seem to want?"

She paused. "I couldn't offer you quid pro quo, but I can tell you I'll get your idea in front of an acquiring executive, and we'll take a look at it."

"But no promises?"

"We'll give it full and fair consideration." She was sincere in that. Just because they'd never commissioned a third-party program for LBS didn't mean they never would.

"And your brothers?" Conrad took a healthy swallow of his new drink. "Are they aware that the scandal is over?"

"They are. They're each involved in the corporation in different ways."

"But not on the media side?"

"Not on a day-to-day basis," said Angelica. "But the family it united." It was a bit of a stretch. There were certainly some fences left to mend, but Angelica was confident her brothers wouldn't say anything publicly that would disparage her father or the family.

"And Jack Reed?" Conrad asked, giving yet another nod to the butler.

Angelica hadn't even touched her second drink. Luckily, while Conrad momentarily turned away, Evan once again deftly switched glasses with her, drinking it himself.

"Jack is completely out of the picture," she said. "There was some confusion about his role at first, but he was also acting on my father's wishes."

Conrad arched a bushy brow. "Your father *wanted* his company to be taken over and split apart?"

The butler returned, and they all exchanged their empty glasses for fresh drinks.

"My father," Angelica admitted with frank honesty, "set it up to test how I would react if that became a possibility."

Conrad cracked a grin. "A wily old coot, was he?"

"I would say so."

Evan joined in. "Everyone passed the test with flying colors. The family pulled together, and Lassiter Media is going to thrive."

"They didn't pull together right away," Conrad noted.

Evan gave a shrug and took a hearty swallow of what was now his fifth glass of scotch. "Nobody does the right thing right away."

Conrad gave a wheezing laugh at that.

"First we look at the angles," Evan continued. "Then we decide what we want. Then we decide what's best. But the last decision is the only one that counts."

Angelica forced herself to take a sip of her drink. She wished the glass contained a liquor she enjoyed. She needed something to counteract her burgeoning appreciation of Evan. He sounded quite sincere in his defense of her behavior.

"And what about you two?" Conrad asked, glancing from one to the other.

"We're friends now," Evan offered simply.

"No, you're not," Conrad countered with conviction, his bushy brows coming together, creasing his forehead.

Angelica stilled, worried they were caught.

"In a relationship like yours," he continued, "you either love each other or you hate each other. There's nothing in between."

"You can't believe what you read in the tabloids," said Evan.

"It's not what I read. It's what I see. Picture after picture tells me you two had it bad." His wrinkled hand gestured back and forth between the two of them. "I'm no fool. You're makin' nice now, but it'll go off the rails in the blink of an eye. The story will hit the tabloids, and this wedding and my mansion will be smack dab in the middle of a scandal."

"You're right," said Evan, and Angelica shot him a look of amazement. But then his hand closed around hers with a reassuring squeeze. "Truth is, we've been thinking about getting back together."

He raised her hand to his lips and gently kissed her knuckles. A familiar buzz of awareness traveled along her arm to her heart, and she had to struggle to mask her reaction.

"You have not," said Conrad. "Nobody keeps a secret like that in this town."

"We do," said Evan, sounding completely convincing. "Look at her, Conrad. I'd have to be a blind fool to give her up."

Conrad's gaze took in every facet of Angelica's appearance. She told herself to hold still and try to look like some kind of 1950s dream girl, the kind you forgave, took back and married, even when she messed up your life.

Conrad finished his drink, and Evan followed suit.

"You've got me there," said Conrad.

"I think you've had enough to drink, sweetheart." Evan lifted the glass from her hand and drank it himself.

Angelica focused on looking calm, serene and in love.

"I'll be damned," said Conrad, his expression relaxing for the first time since they'd arrived.

"I'm no fool," said Evan.

"I guess you're not. So, you're telling me I don't need to worry about wading into a scandal?"

"I'm assuring you this won't blow up in your face."

"What was that date again?"

"Last weekend of the month."

"*This* month?"

"I realize it's short notice. I told you about the fire at the Emerald?"

"We'd need extra staff and security," said Conrad.

"We'll take care of all the details," Evan assured him.

Angelica held her breath.

Conrad nodded his head. "I'll leave the details to you."

"Thank you so much," Angelica reflexively gushed,

reaching out to shake Conrad's hand with both of hers. "Kayla will be so excited."

"Yeah, yeah." Conrad gruffly brushed away the thanks and seemed to mentally withdraw.

"We've imposed on you long enough," said Evan polishing off the last drink. "Thank you for this, sir. Is there a staff member we can contact?"

"Albert will bring you a business card."

The butler, who had remained nearby, came forward to give the card to Evan.

"Goodnight, Conrad." Evan tucked the card into his suit pocket and shook Conrad's hand.

Conrad gave Angelica a parting smile. "I guess I'll be seeing you again soon."

"You will," Angelica agreed. "I'll look forward to it."

Evan put his hand at the small of her back and guided her back through the great room toward the hallway. As soon as the front door was closed behind them, he leaned down to whisper. "You were amazing."

"Are you okay?"

"How do you mean?"

"You drank six single malts."

"Oh, that. Getting him a little drunk seemed like a good strategy, and I couldn't very well throw you to the wolves." Evan blew out a breath as they approached the car. "But I am a little woozy. I think you'd better drive."

"No kidding."

He walked her to the driver's side door, extracting the keys. "Do you know how to drive a stick?"

"I can manage."

"She's peppy," he warned.

Angelica's back was to the car door, and she couldn't help smiling at the warning. "I'll be fine."

Then he went silent, and she suddenly realized just how close to her he was standing. The warmth of his body swirled out to meet her skin. She picked up his familiar scent on the breeze. He smelled good, so good, and she felt herself sway involuntarily toward him. Her hormonal reaction to Evan hadn't changed one bit.

That was bad.

"I mean it," he said in a gravelly voice. "You did great in there."

"So did you," she told him sincerely.

He inched ever so slightly closer. "We make a good team—you and me."

"You're drunk, Evan."

"Maybe a little."

"Your judgment is impaired."

"My judgment is perfect. You're incredible, Angie. And I wanted you just as badly sober as I do now."

Before she realized what was happening, his lips were on hers. Magic exploded inside her brain, colors flashing, music playing, the taste of Evan overwhelming her senses. The kiss went on for long minutes before he finally pulled back.

She was breathless, and not nearly as horrified as she ought to have been. She had to get it together here.

"That did *not* demonstrate good judgment, Evan," she told him tartly, holding out her hand for the car keys.

He just grinned and dropped the keys into her palm. "Sure it did."

The Lassiter Media building's twenty-seventh floor patio, with its adjacent café, was normally open to all the company executives. But today, it was closed for Angelica's private meeting with her brothers and cousin. Together, the four controlled the broader Lassiter conglomerate group.

At her request, they'd agreed to coordinate trips to L.A. Chance and Sage were in from Wyoming, where Chance ran the family's Big Blue ranch and Sage took care of his own business interests. Dylan managed the Lassiter Grill Group.

They were at a dining table beside the fountain as Dylan popped the cork on a bottle of Chateau Montegro, a signature wine of Lassiter Grill. Chance was telling Sage about the adventures of a couple of the ranch cowboys.

Feeling like she needed to clear the air, Angelica broke into the lighthearted story. "Before we go any further, can you please let me apologize?"

They all looked at her, falling silent.

"This isn't a celebration," she reminded Dylan.

She forced herself to look at each of them in turn, Chance with his strong face and ranch-weathered complexion, Dylan with his ready smile and compassionate eyes, Sage with his closed expression and tight rein on his feelings.

"Please let me get this out. I am so profoundly and incredibly sorry for putting you all through this."

Dylan was quick to speak up. "It isn't your fault."

"But it is." She wasn't going to back away from this.

"You got the short end of the stick," said Chance. "The will took us all by surprise. I can't honestly say what I would have done if I'd been shafted like that."

"You'd have walked away," Angelica told her cousin with conviction. She glanced at her brothers as well. "All of you. If J.D. had left you out of his will, you'd have accepted it and walked away."

Sage spoke up. "That's because we wouldn't have been surprised. His relationship with us was a lot more strained than his relationship with you."

"You mean he spoiled me." She was determined to be completely honest here.

"He loved you," said Dylan. "He loved you and you expected, you *knew*, you always knew above everything else that he'd take care of you. And he didn't. Or it looked like he didn't."

"Ultimately, it was his choice," said Angelica. "It was his money, his companies. He was free to leave them to whomever he pleased." She swallowed a catch in her throat. "I should have accepted his decision right away."

Sage reached out and put a hand on her shoulder. "Don't beat yourself up, little sister."

The unexpected endearment made her tear up. Sage wasn't one to demonstrate emotion. "I'm so sorry," she managed.

"Okay," said Dylan, raising the bottle of Chateau Montegro. "You're sorry. It's done. We accept your apology."

Both Sage and Chance nodded with conviction.

"We're family," said Chance. "It's up to us to stick together now."

The obvious love in their expressions made the weight slowly lift from Angelica's shoulders. Her tears dried, and she managed a weak smile.

Dylan began pouring the wine.

"I don't know why he even left me the twenty-five percent of Lassiter Media," Sage said to Angelica. "I'm busy running Spence Enterprises. I'll sign the shares over to you anytime you want."

She shook her head. "No, you won't. I'm through second-guessing our father. You're a significant shareholder in Lassiter Media, and you're staying that way. If I had to guess, I'd say he wanted to make sure you felt like part of this family. Besides, I want to be able to come to you for advice."

Sage grinned. "You don't need any of my advice on Lassiter Media. Evan's the one who—" He abruptly stopped himself, looking apologetic.

"You're allowed to say his name," said Angelica.

"Have you spoken to him? I mean, since the day you took over?" asked Dylan, handing her a glass of the red wine.

"I have," she confirmed. "We talked yesterday."

All three men looked surprised by the news. They waited for her to elaborate.

"We're standing up for Kayla and Matt," she explained. "They're getting married at the end of the month."

There was a further beat of silence all around. All three men looked decidedly worried.

"It's fine," she assured them.

"How can it be fine?" asked Dylan.

She waved away their concern. "We're friends—" She stopped herself, realizing that lying to her family was ridiculous. "Okay, we're not friends. We've hurt each other in too many ways to ever even contemplate forgiveness. But we can pretend to be friends—we *have* to pretend to be friends—for Kayla and Matt's sake."

"You want us to talk to him?" asked Sage.

Angelica fought a bubble of laughter. "And say what?"

"If he steps out of line," growled Chance.

"Stop it," she ordered. "You guys like Evan. You've always liked Evan." She straightened the silverware in front of her, telling herself it was vital to keep the honesty flowing. "There were times when you liked him better than you liked me."

"Never," said Dylan.

"It's fine," she assured them again. "It's going to be just fine." Her voice went softer. "But, thank you. Thank you for caring, and thank you for supporting me."

Dylan raised his glass, and they all followed suit. "This is long overdue. To J.D."

"To J.D.," they echoed.

"To Dad," Angelica whispered, her heart beginning to heal as she took a first sip.

Three

"Why are you even still here?" Evan asked Deke as they slowed to a walk on the beach pathway north of the Santa Monica Pier.

"I'm helping," Deke answered through labored breaths. He angled his way through the colorful afternoon crowd of tourists, buskers and rollerbladers, going toward the slushy kiosk. They'd ended their jog a couple of blocks from Evan's building.

"You're not helping at all." Evan followed along without complaint because he was incredibly thirsty.

"I got a hot lead this morning."

"*I* got a hot lead this morning. You just answered my phone."

"I provided excellent service. Two large lemon mangos," Deke said to the kiosk clerk.

"How do you know I want lemon mango?"

"You want something else?"

"I don't care." As long as it was cold and wet, Evan would be happy.

Deke handed a twenty to the clerk. "Then why are you griping?"

"I want a little control over my life."

"You want a little control over Angelica Lassiter."

"Say what?" How had Angie gotten into the conversation?

"You're sexually frustrated, and you're taking it out on me."

The clerk smirked as he handed Deke his change.

"I'm not sexually frustrated," Evan said in a loud voice, as much for the clerk's benefit as anything else. His lack of a sex life was purely by choice.

"You want Angelica. You can't have her. So you're pissy."

"Hey, I kissed her. Just last night. And she kissed me back."

The clerk had turned away to operate the slushy machine, which was chugging out the lemon mango, so Evan couldn't tell if he'd heard the brag.

"The hell you say," said Deke.

"I say."

"Where'd you kiss her?"

"Conrad Norville's."

"Is that above or below the waist?"

"Ha, ha."

"So, what does that mean?" Deke asked, going serious again.

Evan shrugged, already regretting having shared the information. "I don't know," he admitted.

It meant nothing. He was a fool to have mentioned it. He'd all but forced that kiss on Angie. Her return kiss had been reflexive, an obvious result of shock and surprise. It might have been fantastic, but she hadn't meant it. Afterward, she'd been nothing but annoyed.

The clerk slid the slushy drinks across the counter, and they each took one.

"When are you seeing her again?" asked Deke as they turned away.

"In an hour. The Emerald Wave faxed Matt and Kayla's plans for the wedding so we could pick up the ball. We'll need to contact the florist, the bakery, the musicians. And we need to check out a new caterer."

"Does Matt know about the fire?"

"He does now. I finally got a text from him this morning. But it looks like they'll be a couple more days getting back." Evan plopped down on a bench facing the ocean and took a long, satisfying drink.

Deke sat down next to him. "You're not meeting her at Lassiter Media, are you?"

"Good grief, no," said Evan. The Lassiter Media building was the last place on earth he wanted to be.

"You want company?"

Evan's first reaction was to grin. "You think I need protection from Angie?"

"More like she needs protection from you."

"It's all under control."

Evan had everything in perspective. He just needed to keep his emotional reaction to Angie separate from his intellectual understanding of the situation. And he could do that.

Her lack of trust in him had destroyed any chance they had as a couple. But that didn't mean she wasn't attractive. She was just as gorgeous and sexy as she'd ever been. And the fact that he could picture her naked in such vivid and astonishing detail was to be completely expected.

But he could handle it. He had no choice but to handle it.

"You just told me you kissed her," said Deke.

"It was nothing."

"Kissing your ex-fiancée is not nothing."

"It was a slipup. She was standing there. I was standing there…" Evan struggled to keep his mind from going back to that incredible moment.

"And if she's 'standing there' again today?"

"She won't be."

Deke gave a choked laugh.

"You know what I mean." Evan took another drink.

The sun was hot on his sweat-damp head, burning along the back of his neck. The shrieks of children on the sand swirled around him, while the moist, salt air sat heavily in his lungs.

"I'm coming with you," Deke announced. "And afterward we're hitting a club or two and dancing with some new, hot women."

Evan was about to refuse. But he realized Deke was right. He had to nip this in the bud. Angie was his past, not his future. Once they were done with Matt and Kayla's wedding, they were going their separate ways. Letting himself fantasize about her would only delay his recovery.

"Fine," he agreed. "Suit yourself."

"Thanks for helping out with this," Angelica said to Tiffany as she drove her ice-blue sports car into the parking lot of the Terrace Bistro where she and Evan had agreed to meet.

"Why are you thanking me?" Tiffany asked. "It's my job. Kayla needs me. Besides, there's no way I'm letting you face Evan alone."

"I faced him alone last night," Angelica pointed out.

Not that she was looking forward to doing it again. Their kiss last night had completely rattled her. It should have felt awkward. It should have felt strange. She should have recoiled from the feel of his hands and the taste of his lips.

But it had felt familiar. It had felt like coming home.

"You okay, Angie?" Tiffany reached out to touch her arm.

"I'm perfectly fine." Angelica shut off the ignition and set the car's emergency brake. Then a wave of anxiety hit her, and she latched her hands on to the steering wheel, gripping hard for a second.

"Angie?"

"I'm over him." She released her grip on the steering wheel. "And he's definitely over me. Let's go."

"He kissed you, didn't he?" Tiffany had already heard the entire story.

"That was an… I don't know what that was. But it wasn't

a regular kiss. He was making some kind of debating point or maybe a power play, or he was mocking me."

"Well, I'm here for you if he tries anything over dinner."

"Thank you," Angelica told her sincerely. "He won't. And I don't care one way or the other. He's just another guy to me."

"If you say so." Tiffany sounded doubtful.

"I say so," Angelica responded with conviction. She pocketed her keys and opened the car door.

The two women made their way across the parking lot to the non-descript, little café. Inside, Angelica spotted Evan at a corner table. The second his gaze met hers, her stomach fluttered with anticipation, and all her hopes of pretending he was just another guy flew out the window. This was Evan. He was never going to be just another guy.

A moment later, she realized he wasn't alone.

"Who's *that*?" Tiffany whispered from behind her.

"Deke?" Angelica asked the question out loud, quickening her steps. She had only met Evan's college friend Deke a few times, but she'd always liked him. He was slightly shorter than Evan and had dark hair. He was very handsome, and one of the smartest people Angelica had ever met.

He came to his feet, giving her a broad smile. "Angelica." He pulled her into a brief hug that felt entirely natural.

"What are you doing in L.A.?" she asked.

He shrugged. "I got a little restless." His gaze went past her to abruptly stop on Tiffany.

Angelica quickly introduced them. "This is Tiffany. She's Kayla's other bridesmaid."

Deke held out his hand to greet Tiffany, and Angelica quickly stepped out of the way. She realized too late that the action put her in position to sit next to Evan on the bench seat of the booth. Doing anything to switch back would look ridiculously awkward. Besides, Deke was already motioning Tiffany in next to him.

Resigned, Angelica sat down.

"I see you brought reinforcements," Evan noted in an undertone.

"As did you." She settled her purse on the bench seat as a barrier between them.

"Deke's staying with me for a few days."

"In Pasadena?"

"I sold the house in Pasadena."

The words took her by surprise, and she automatically glanced at him. "You did? When? Why?"

"Last week."

"But, you loved that house."

"At the moment, I need the money more than I need a big house."

"But you have—"

"I am not using his money, Angie."

"You'd take a loss on principle?"

"I didn't take a loss. But, yes, *I'd* take a loss on principle."

"What's that supposed to mean," she hissed under her breath as Tiffany and Deke got settled.

Evan handed her a printout on Emerald Wave stationery. "It means, unlike certain other people, I stick to my principles even when it's inconvenient."

"I stuck to *my* principles." Which were, at least in part, to ensure the health and security of Lassiter Media.

"Principles like respecting your father?" he drawled.

"Evan," Tiffany put in smoothly from across the table. "You should shut up now."

Deke gave a muted chuckle.

A waiter appeared at the table. "Good evening."

Angelica gratefully switched her attention to the man.

"Our most popular themes are Mediterranean, southwest and continental." The man handed around some sheets of paper. "I'll give you a few minutes to discuss it, and then I'd be happy to talk about wine pairings for your choices."

Angelica shot Tiffany a confused glance. They had to agree on a theme? What kind of a restaurant was this? Why couldn't they just order from the menu?

"Thank you," said Evan. "We'll let you know what we decide."

"Have you been here before?" Angelica asked him as the waiter stepped away.

"Never." He arranged three sheets of paper in front of him. "But our options were limited at this late date."

"It's a Wednesday." How busy could Malibu restaurants be? It was only five-thirty in the evening.

He gave her a confused look. "I mean our catering options for the wedding."

She blinked. Then she glanced down at the papers in front of them. They listed price points per guest and per platter.

"These are catering menus," she observed.

"Can't get one past you."

"I thought we were here for dinner. I thought you were bringing the Emerald Wave information for us to discuss."

"I am. I did. But we're also sampling the caterer's menu."

Tiffany jumped in. "That sounds like fun."

"I'm game," said Deke. "Not to brag, but I excel at eating."

Tiffany smiled as she gave Deke a sidelong glance.

"You could have told me," Angelica, embarrassed by her own confusion, said to Evan.

"I thought I did tell you when we talked on the phone. Maybe you just didn't listen. Mediterranean, southwest or continental."

Angelica didn't exactly believe him, but she let it go, scanning the catering menus.

"Continental has my vote," said Tiffany.

"I'd be happier if we knew what Kayla wanted."

"I finally got a voice mail from Matt in response to my text," said Evan. "He says thanks. He trusts our judgment. And they'll appreciate anything we can do before they get back. The connection was pretty bad, because I think he said something about the moat being flooded."

"The *moat*?"

"The only logical explanation I could come up with is that the retreat is at a castle somewhere. I know there's a pretty big storm off the North Sea. The upshot is they won't be able to get home for a few more days. We're on our own."

"I agree with Tiffany," said Deke.

Evan glanced up. "Of course you agree with Tiffany. You're flirting with Tiffany." He looked pointedly at her. "Watch out for this guy."

She grinned.

"Southwest is a bit overdone lately," Angelica noted. And the décor at Conrad's mansion definitely lent itself to something a little highbrow.

"Matt's not a huge fan of Mediterranean," Evan put in. "Does that settle it?"

"Sure," said Angelica. "Let's go with continental."

"So, old world wines?"

"Bite your tongue," said Angelica. "California wines, for sure."

Evan smiled without looking at her. He knew full well the Lassiter family had many close friends in the wine business in Napa Valley.

"Are you *trying* to pick a fight with her?" Deke asked him.

Evan seemed to be doing his best to look offended. "I can't make a joke?"

Tiffany put up her hand to signal the waiter. "This seems like a great time to get the wine tasting underway."

"I like the way you think," Deke muttered.

After some consultation with the waiter, they chose several wines to taste along with a selection of appetizers, entrees and desserts from the continental menu.

Despite the rather humble surroundings of the restaurant, the food turned out to be delicious.

Angelica bit into a warm brie and smoked trout appetizer, enfolded in phyllo pastry and garnished with a light herb paste.

"Oh," she groaned, setting the remainder of the morsel down on her plate to savor the mouthful. "This is the best one yet."

"Try the shrimp," said Tiffany. "Oh, man. I'm getting stuffed, but I just can't stop."

"I need some real food," said Evan.

"Get them to bring you the duck or the lamb," Angelica suggested. "But I think I'm going to have to trust you on how those taste. I couldn't possibly eat anymore."

"You'd actually trust me on something?" asked Evan, a lilt to his tone.

She turned to rebuke him for the sarcasm, but then she caught the sparkle in his eyes. She realized she had to stop being so touchy. He'd always had a dry sense of humor. She used to enjoy it.

"So long as you don't try to steal what's rightfully mine," she countered.

In answer, he snagged the remaining bite of brie and smoked trout from her plate, popping it in his mouth.

"Hey!" she protested.

"Guess you shouldn't have trusted me after all. Wow, this is good. Definitely add that to the list."

"You stole my trout."

"You left it unguarded."

"You said I could trust you." She knew she should be annoyed, but she was only barely able to keep from laughing.

"I believe you were the one who offered to trust me."

"Clearly, I was wrong about that."

"Clearly."

She sniffed. "Well, you owe me some trout."

"I'll trade you for some duckling."

"Are you ordering the duckling?" asked Deke. "Then I'll try the veal."

Angelica glanced at the menu. "You mean the duck flambé? With orange brandy?"

"That's the one," said Evan.

"You got yourself a trade." She was about to shake on it, then quickly realized it was a mistake, and redirected her hand to her wineglass, lifting it and taking a sip of the rich merlot.

Evan smirked. He reached below the table between them, squeezing her other hand. She nearly inhaled her wine.

He leaned close, muttering in an undertone as Deke commented to Tiffany about the stuffed mushrooms. "It's okay to touch me, Angie."

At that moment, Evan's fingertips brushed the hem of her skirt, contacting her bare thigh. They both instantly stilled. Arousal radiated along her leg, electrifying her skin, contracting her muscles.

"Orgasmic," Tiffany declared.

Angelica whimpered under her breath.

Evan's warm hand curled open, his palm spreading across her thigh, sliding ever so slightly beneath her skirt.

"Please," she managed to whisper.

"Something wrong?" Tiffany asked her, looking concerned.

"Nothing," she managed, distracting herself with another swallow of the wine. She shifted, but Evan's hand moved with her.

Deke signaled the waiter, asking the man for the duck and the veal.

Evan leaned toward her, his voice a ragged whisper in her ear. "Tell me to stop."

She tried. She opened her mouth, but the words didn't come out.

His hand slipped higher, and her grip tightened on the wine glass.

"Angie?" Tiffany's voice penetrated the haze inside her brain.

"Hmmm?" she managed.

"I said do you have a preference for desserts?"

"Uh. No."

"Torte? Éclairs? Maybe cheesecake?"

"Sure. Yeah."

Evan's fingertips swirled lightly against her skin. The sensation took her back months in time. For some reason, she remembered a particular morning when they'd lounged in bed at his house in Pasadena. It had been pouring rain, and he'd made hot chocolate, lacing it with coffee liqueur.

"Maybe the pecan tarts?" asked Tiffany.

"Okay," Angelica managed.

Tiffany peered at her strangely. "You look flushed. Are you having an allergic reaction?" Her glance darted from dish to dish. "Were there almonds in something?"

"No, no." Angelica put in quickly. "I'm good. I'm fine." She put her hand down on top of Evan's. She'd intended to push him away, but somehow it didn't happen. Instead she pressed down on his hand, pushing it harder against her thigh.

"The chocolate truffles," said Evan. "Get them to bring some of the chocolate truffles."

Tiffany smiled. "I *love* chocolate. It's so richly decadent."

Evan's touch was richly decadent, and indulgent, and Angelica had to stop him.

"Are you dating anyone?" Deke asked Tiffany.

"Seriously?" asked Evan. "You're hitting on her during dinner?"

"I'm asking her out," said Deke. "There's a big difference."

"I can tell the difference," Tiffany offered breezily. "And he's hitting on me."

Deke pulled back in his seat in mock offense, his hand on his heart. "You wound me deeply."

As Tiffany answered back, Evan leaned in close to Angelica's ear again. "In case you're wondering, I'm also hitting on you."

His words gave her the strength to tug his hand away. He gave in easily, but she was left quivering.

Evan knew it was his turn to make sure Angelica got home safely. By the time they made it through the all the wines, she was in no condition to drive, and Tiffany was probably over the limit as well. He paid the bill and slid his keys across the table to Deke. Then he held out his hands for Angelica's keys.

"I'm fine to—" She stopped herself. "You're right. I'm not driving anywhere. But I can call a driver."

"Don't be ridiculous. It'll take them until midnight just to get here."

"They're on call for a reason."

"And I'm already here. I trusted you to drive my car, and it's a whole lot more expensive than yours."

"Can you drive an automatic?" she asked, humor lurking in her slightly glassy eyes.

"I'll manage." He flicked his gaze to Tiffany. "We'll have to put you in a cab."

The sports car was a two-seater.

"I'll take her home," Deke offered.

"Oh, no you don't," said Evan.

"You'll love Evan's convertible," Deke said to Tiffany.

She looked at Evan. "I'm more worried about you with Angie than I am about Deke with me."

"Seriously?" Evan asked, honestly offended. "How well do you know me?"

Tiffany studied his expression for a critical moment. "I don't want you fighting with her."

"I'll be a perfect gentleman," said Evan.

Truth was, fighting with Angie was the very last thing on his mind. Seducing her, now that was the real danger.

But he could absolutely control himself. His hand might still be warm where he'd caressed her thigh, and he might remember the unique, arousing texture of her skin, but he was keeping it in context. He *had* to keep it all in context.

"You'll be okay with him?" Tiffany asked Angie.

"I have to get my car home somehow."

"You're not drunk?"

"I'm not drunk. I'm merely over the legal limit from doing my duty as a bridesmaid."

"Fair enough," said Tiffany. "I on the other hand did my duty with the dessert." She popped the last chocolate truffle into her mouth.

"How *do* you stay so slim?" asked Deke.

"Give the compliments a rest," she responded with a laugh. "They're not going to work."

Watching the exchange, Evan couldn't help feeling envious of Deke. He suddenly wished he and Angie had just met tonight, that they had no baggage between them. If that were the case, he'd also be putting on a full-court press.

"You ready?" he asked her, resisting the urge to smooth stray wisps of hair away from her forehead.

She reached for the purse between them. "I really didn't think this through."

"I'll get you home safe," he told her.

She gave him a nod of agreement and slid from the booth. The two couples separated at the bottom of the café steps. Evan settled Angie into the passenger seat before starting her car and pulling onto the highway.

As he drove, he struggled to push away the memory of her warm skin. But instead, he found himself wondering what she'd thought. When he'd caressed her thigh, she hadn't immediately pushed him away.

Maybe she was too shocked by his behavior to react. Or maybe she'd been sitting there fuming mad. He knew nothing good could come of bringing it up again. But that didn't mean he could stop it from ticking through his mind.

He made it fifteen silent minutes down the Pacific Coast Highway before he cracked. He wheeled into a dark parking lot overlooking the surf and the moonlit night.

"What?" Angie was clearly confused by the unexpected stop, glancing around outside.

He angled his body to face her. "Should I apologize here?"

Her jaw went lax in obvious shock, and her eyes went round in the dashboard glow. "You'd actually do that?" she asked in an awed whisper.

It took him a moment to realize what she was thinking. She thought he was talking about how he'd gone along with J.D.'s will. For some reason, she'd guessed he meant the big apology, the one where he told her he'd been wrong all those months, that she was justified in not trusting him, and that the problems between them were his fault, not hers.

That was never going to happen.

"For what I did in the restaurant," he clarified.

"The…oh. Okay." She schooled her features and glanced away from him.

"I didn't do it to upset you." Half his brain was telling him to shut up already, while the other half seemed hell-bent on ploughing forward. "It was an accident. Well, at first. But then…you didn't seem to mind."

"I minded a whole lot."

"You didn't stop me."

She looked at him again. "You took me by surprise."

"I took me by surprise too," he admitted.

They both fell silent, and the air seemed to thicken inside the dim car. His gaze moved to her full lips, and her taste from last night invaded his senses. He wanted to kiss her again, wanted it very badly.

"Evan, don't."

"Don't what?" He hadn't made a single move here.

"I can see what you're thinking."

"You can read my mind, Angie? Really?"

"You're remembering what it was like between us." She swallowed. "You remember it being good."

"It *was* good."

"Sex is always good."

Her words were like a bucket of cold water. "*Always*?"

"Evan, don't."

"You've had a lot of sex lately, have you?"

She smoothed the hem of her skirt. "That's none of your business."

"With who?"

"Stop."

Hard anger invaded his stomach, turning his voice to a growl. "Who, Angie? Who've you been sleeping with? Was it Jack Reed?"

"Jack's with Becca now."

"Doesn't mean he wasn't ever with you."

"I am *not* having this conversation." She abruptly swung open the door.

He leaned across the car, reaching for her, but she slipped out too quickly, slamming the car door firmly behind her. He was out his side in a shot, pacing his way to her.

"Tell me the truth," he demanded. It wasn't the first time he'd wondered about Jack Reed. And it wasn't the first time he'd wanted to take the man apart.

She glared defiantly up at him, her back against the car. "Why? Why would you even care?"

"That's a yes."

"It's *not* a yes," she retorted.

"How long?" he asked, his tone deceptively soft. "How long after you left my bed were you in his?"

"I never slept with Jack."

"I don't believe you."

"Believe whatever you want, Evan. But I have never lied to you, and I'm not about to start now. I haven't slept with anyone since we broke up." She gave a slightly hysterical laugh. "When would I have time for a relationship? And you, of all people, *you*, Evan—" she jabbed a finger against his chest "—should know I don't just jump into any man's bed."

He trapped her hand, holding it against his thudding heart. "Nobody?"

Her eyes were black as the night around them. "Nobody. And I'm insulted that you asked."

"You're a beautiful woman, Angie." He wasn't entirely sure if it was an explanation for his suspicions or an observation in the moment. Every time he saw her, he was blown away by her beauty. "Men must hit on you all the time."

"I understand how to say the word no, Evan."

"Yeah?" He felt himself swaying forward.

"Yeah," she told him with conviction.

"Then tell me no."

To be fair, he didn't actually give her time to answer. His lips were on hers again before she could even draw a breath. In the back of his mind, he realized he had to stop doing this. He had no right to kiss her, no right to touch her, no right in the world to ask about her sex life. But right and wrong seemed to fly out the window when she was near.

Before he knew it, she was in his arms, their kiss deepening. Somehow, she had imprinted on him. The memory of making love to her was burned into his spinal column. He knew to wrap one arm around her waist, bury his fingers in her hair, caress the back of her neck, tease her tongue with the tip of his own. Her little moan was familiar to his ears, while the scent of her hair took him back in time.

The next move was his hand at her waist, slipping under her blouse, rising up to cup the lace of her bra.

"We can't," she cried, pushing her hands against his chest and turning her head away.

He ordered himself to let go, but it took his body a moment to react.

"We can't let that happen." She pressed herself back against the car.

He eased off, putting some space between them, his breath ragged. "I didn't plan it."

There was an edge of hysteria to her voice. "You think I did?"

"No. No. Of course not. I'm only saying—" After all they'd been through, he shouldn't want to make her feel better about the slipup, but for some reason he did. "I'm only saying the physical attraction is still there. It doesn't have to mean anything."

"It doesn't mean anything." She paused. "Okay, it means we have to be careful."

"We do," he agreed. They seemed all but combustible when they got close to each other.

He also realized that the kiss had answered his original question. There was no need to apologize. He tried to rein in his ego, but he failed.

He voiced his suspicions. "You liked it. That's why you didn't stop me. You liked my hand on your thigh."

"I did not," she snapped.

"You said you wouldn't lie."

"I told you, it shocked me."

"But you liked it," he challenged.

She looked him straight in the eyes. "Like I said, we have to be careful."

She might not have confirmed it. But she hadn't denied it.

He couldn't help the self-satisfied grin that spread across his face.

Four

"Angelica?" Her brother Dylan's voice came over the speakerphone on the meeting room table. "Is there something you want to tell us?"

Angelica had temporarily set herself up in a comfortable meeting room on the twenty-eighth floor of the Lassiter Media building, leaving the top floor boardroom and J.D.'s office free for the renovators.

"Tell you what? And who is us?" she asked as she continued to page through a financial report.

"The *us* is me and Sage. The *what* is the article in the *Weekly Break* newspaper about you and Evan getting back together."

Angelica snatched up the telephone receiver, glancing worriedly at the open meeting room door. "*What*?"

"That's what I'm asking you," Dylan responded mildly.

"I don't know where they'd get that." Her mind flipped frantically back to last night when she'd kissed Evan at the parking lot on the highway. Could a reporter have possibly gotten a shot of them in that moment? "Is there a picture?"

"Is there a picture?" Dylan parroted. "Are you telling me there might possibly be a picture?"

"There can't be a picture," she lied. "Unless it's an old

one. You know, maybe with a current newspaper Photo-shopped into it."

"It's not a ransom demand."

"I realize that." She didn't know what else to say.

"Angie?" Dylan's tone was searching. "What's going on?"

"*Nothing* is going on."

She caught a flash of movement in the corner of her eye and glanced up to see Evan in the doorway, a copy of the *Weekly Break* in his hand.

"I have to go," she said to Dylan.

"Angie."

"I have a meeting." Her eyes locked with Evan's. "It's nothing. They've made up a story is all."

"Are you sure, because we'd all be very happy—"

"Goodbye, Dylan." She quickly hung up the phone.

"You heard?" asked Evan, walking into the meeting room.

"You shouldn't be here."

She came to her feet, crossing the room to close the door.

"You might not want to close that," he observed.

"Speculation is probably better than having them over-hear our conversation. What happened? What does it say?" She reflexively put a hand to her forehead. "Oh, man, how is Conrad going to react to this?"

Evan tossed the paper onto the top of the meeting table. "I think Conrad's the source."

She glanced down to see a damning headline on the front page. There was a picture of them, but thank goodness it was from last year.

"They didn't catch us last night?" she asked, spinning the paper right-side up in her direction.

"Now, *that's* the kind of thing you don't want people to overhear."

She frowned at him. "You know what I mean."

"There's no new photo," he confirmed. "But an unnamed source quoted me as saying I'd be a blind fool to give you up."

Angelica closed her eyes for a long moment. "Conrad."

"Unless it was the butler."

She opened her eyes to look at Evan. "Butlers get fired for a lot less than that."

"My money's definitely on Conrad."

"But why would he do that? He said he wanted the Lassiters to stay *out* of the tabloids."

"Maybe he's calling our bluff."

"No." But she hesitated. "You think?" She glanced down at the article. "What would be his motivation?"

"I don't pretend to have the first clue about what makes that man tick."

"What are we supposed to do now?" They couldn't let this stand. But they couldn't let Conrad know the truth either. Kayla's wedding was at stake.

"We may have to ride it out."

Angelica did not like the sound of that. She dropped back into her chair, voice going low, trepidation rising. "What do you mean, ride it out?"

"I mean..." He pulled out a chair across from her and sat down. "We don't deny anything to anybody until after the ceremony."

"And let the world think we're getting back together?"

Evan shrugged.

She shook her head. "Uh-uh. No way."

"I'm not saying it's a good answer."

"We can't do that."

"The alternative is to tell Conrad we lied."

She continued shaking her head. "We can't do that either."

"Then tell me the third option."

She frantically searched her brain. But there was no third option. She brought the side of her fist down on the paper. "How did we not see this coming?"

"We never guessed he'd go to the tabloids."

"We shouldn't have assumed he'd keep it a secret." She could have kicked herself for being so stupid.

"Well, I was drunk," Evan drawled.

"This isn't funny," she snapped in return.

"I don't think it's funny, Angie. But nobody's going to die from it either. It's two-and-a-half weeks. And then we're done. We fake a breakup and walk away."

"I am not going to lie to my brothers." It would be bad enough having strangers think they were a couple.

"I understand."

"I mean, after all we've been through. We just got back on an even keel. I can't possibly do that to them, Evan."

He seemed to ponder for a moment. "I do understand. Trouble is, Sage can't lie to Colleen and Dylan can't lie to Jenna."

"Of course they can't," she agreed.

"And you want Chance to have to lie to Felicia?"

Angelica set her jaw.

"Exactly how big do you think we can make the conspiracy before somebody accidentally trips up?"

She felt her throat close up. No matter which way she turned, somebody got hurt. "I can't do this."

His tone turned gentle. "You don't have to lie, Angie."

"How do I not have to lie? How can I possibly not have to lie?"

"Answer me this. If I was to come to you on bended knee, telling you I was sorry, that it was all my fault, that I thought we should give it another try, would you dismiss the idea out of hand, or would you at least think about it?"

It was a ridiculous scenario. "You are never, *ever* going to do that."

"I'm not," he agreed. "But if you were to come to me on bended knee, telling me you were sorry, that it was all your fault, and that you thought we should give it another try, I'm pretty sure I'd at least think about it."

"That's your loophole?"

"So, when you say to someone—*if you were* to say to someone—that we both knew we had a lot of issues to work through, that the chances were slim, but we had discussed getting back together, it wouldn't be a lie."

"Technically, no," she allowed.

"Precisely no."

Her chest had gone heavy with pain. "And that's what you want us to do? You want us to let the entire world think we're giving it another shot?"

"Think about the benefits, all of the benefits. There's Conrad, of course, and the wedding venue. But also Kayla and Matt's emotional comfort. They won't have to tippy-toe around us. Everybody at the wedding will be more comfortable. You and I won't feel like we're under a microscope."

That was exactly how she'd expected to feel at the wedding.

"It's traditional for the best man and maid of honor to dance together," Evan continued. "Can you imagine what the guests would be thinking? 'Is she frowning? Is he grimacing? What are they saying to each other? Are they fighting?'"

"You've given this a lot of thought." She hated to admit that she had as well. She was trying desperately not to dread the reception, but she was losing the battle.

"I like to think I'm a realist, Angie."

"You promised to call me Angelica."

He gave a small smile. "I don't remember promising. But now that we're thinking about getting back together, you'll have to put up with it for a couple more weeks."

She glanced back down at the headline. "You really think we should do this?"

"It'll be over before you know it."

***

"What, exactly do you think you're doing?" Deke asked as he strode into Evan's office in Santa Monica.

"Manual labor," Evan answered, holding one of the metal brackets for a shelving unit against the wall, his cordless drill groaning as he anchored the screws.

The door banged shut behind Deke, the blinds rattling with what was becoming a familiar sound. "I read the tabloid story."

"I had nothing to do with it." Evan reached for another screw on the counter beside him.

"You're quoted in it."

"Don't believe everything you read."

"So, you're not getting back together with Angie?"

Evan thought through his words. "We're talking. We're thinking. We're spending a little time together."

There was a moment of silence. "Are you using recreational drugs?"

Evan snorted a non-reply.

"Seriously, Evan. Have you completely lost your mind?"

"No."

"Then, *what the hell?*"

Evan immediately realized that deceiving Deke was never going to work. The only way he could pull this off was if Deke was in on the ruse. His friend knew him too well, and Deke would be around him too much this month to get away with lying.

He gave in. "Fine. Okay. It was a ruse to get Conrad to let us use his mansion."

It seemed to take Deke a moment to process the statement. "You told Conrad you were getting back together with Angie."

"It was the only way."

"It was a stupid way."

Evan smiled to himself, lining up the final screw. He

drilled it firmly through the bracket and into the wall. "Well, it's too late to turn back now."

Deke crossed his arms over his chest. "I was your first phone call. Remember? I know the state you were in the day you and Angie split up."

Evan's hand tightened on the drill grip. "I remember."

"It was a bad day, buddy."

"No kidding," Evan repeated.

It wasn't a day he talked about. He refused to dwell on it. He simply pointed his life forward and took it one step at a time. He turned back to the counter and set down the drill.

Deke took a step forward. "You can't go through that again."

Evan retrieved a box cutter from his tool kit and set to work on the cardboard box that held the wooden shelves. "We're faking it, Deke. Pretending to like each other. We won't break up again, because we're not getting back together."

Deke followed Evan's lead, locating another cutter and slicing through the tape at the opposite end of the long box. "You still like her. Hell, I think you still love her."

Evan's heart gave a little lurch inside his chest. "It's impossible to love someone who doesn't trust you."

"Maybe." Deke sounded skeptical as he peeled back the box flaps.

"There's no maybe about it. I don't love her." Evan pulled away the packing tape and opened the box. The cherrywood planks were wrapped in bubble plastic.

"It's not an on-off switch."

"It's a do-don't switch," Evan responded with conviction. "And I don't."

"I saw the way you looked at her last night."

"That was lust."

"So, you admit you're still attracted to her?"

Evan knew there was no point in denying it to Deke or

to himself. "I may not be in love with her, but I remember what she looks like naked."

Deke cracked a smile at the answer. "I hear you. I'm still trying to find out what Tiffany looks like naked."

Evan lifted the first shelf from the box. "Good luck with that."

"She's hot. And she's funny. And she's killer smart."

"Angie's going to warn her about you."

"What's to warn? I'm a perfectly nice, perfectly rich, perfectly decent-looking guy."

Evan placed the shelf on the top bracket. "With a perfect track record of short, meaningless relationships."

"See, that's why I worry about you. You claim it's lust, but you buy into the whole hearts-and-flowers thing. You, my friend, have a perfect track record of long, meaningful relationships."

"I did it *once*," Evan pointed out.

"With Angie."

"Your point?"

"I don't believe you're over her."

"I am." It wasn't like Evan had a choice.

"You're going to get hurt."

"I can take care of myself." Evan might still be attracted to Angie, but he was a realist. He was going into this thing with his eyes wide open.

Deke handed him the next shelf. "Just so you know, when it all goes bad and you feel like you have to call in the cavalry—"

"Yeah, yeah. Don't call you."

"What? No. *Do* call me. At least I'm experienced now. We'll head over to Italy and rent a chateau on the Mediterranean. Jeez, Evan. Just because you're stupid, doesn't mean I don't have your back."

Evan couldn't help but chuckle. "Thanks, man. But it won't be necessary."

"We'll see."

The office door swung open, and both men turned toward the sound.

"Lex?" Evan spoke first, astonished that their former roommate was standing in his doorway. "I thought you were in London."

"I heard you were starting over." Lex glanced around the disorganized office. "You do know you can hire carpenters and decorators to do this kind of thing."

"You can?" Evan dusted his hands on his blue jeans as he rounded the end of the reception counter.

"There's this thing called Handyman Listing on the internet.…"

Evan grinned as he reached out to shake Lex's hand, clasping his shoulder at the same time. He hadn't seen his friend in over a year. "I'm keeping myself busy. What on earth are you doing in L.A.?"

"Asanti's holding some corporate meetings in New York." Lex nodded to Deke and reached over to shake. "Hey, man. Good to see you again."

The answer was ridiculous. It was clear to Evan Lex was hiding something.

He pressed. "So, you were just on the continent and thought you'd stop by?"

"Something like that."

Evan turned to Deke. "You called him."

"Of course I called him. You weren't going to call him."

"Because there was nothing to tell him."

"You lost your job," said Deke. "You lost your girl. And you're all but destitute."

Evan knew this had gone far enough. "I'm hardly destitute."

Both men raised their eyebrows.

"Seriously," said Evan. "You two want to compare the zeros in our bank accounts?"

Lex laughed.

But Evan wasn't finished. "Deke might have a share in all those technology patents, but I know how to invest." He looked at Lex. "And all you have is a salary." Admittedly, it was probably a very good salary.

"And stock options," said Lex.

"Yeah?" Deke asked with obvious interest.

Lex nodded. "In fact, I'm seriously thinking about cashing them in and buying the Sagittarius."

"Say what?" asked Deke.

"The Sagittarius Resort?" Evan pointed in the general direction of the Pacific Ocean. "*That* Sagittarius?"

Lex nodded.

The five-star complex had close to a thousand rooms and sat on a stunning stretch of beach north of Malibu. It was one of the crown jewels of the California tourism industry.

"I figure it could be the start of a new chain," said Lex.

"You can afford it?" asked Deke.

"I'd need a partner. Maybe two partners." He sent a meaningful glance in Evan's direction.

"Oh, no, no." Evan took a step backward, glancing at Deke, knowing a setup when he saw one. "I don't know how you two lost your collective minds, but you are not riding in here to rescue me. I'm fine. I am completely fine, professionally, financially and romantically."

"What makes you think this is about you?" asked Lex.

"Of course it's about me." Evan was equal parts touched and horrified that his friends would suggest such an outlandish scheme.

"This is the first I'm hearing about the Sagittarius," said Deke.

Evan didn't know whether to believe him or not.

"I'd have to be a silent partner," Deke continued, looking for all the world like he was taking the idea seriously. "I don't have time for any day-to-day responsibilities. Then again, I wouldn't need to draw a salary either."

"No problem," Lex responded. "I can run a hotel with my eyes closed. Evan will be in charge of international expansion. You just pony up with a check."

Deke was nodding thoughtfully.

"Stop this," Evan demanded, glancing from one man to the other. "You two have completely over-estimated the magnitude of my problems."

"It's not all about you, Evan," said Deke.

"Ha," Evan barked.

"What is *with* him?" Lex asked Deke.

"He isn't over Angie yet."

"I am absolutely over—"

"Well, *get* over Angie," said Lex. "And think logically here. Tell me that the three of us going into business together would not be an absolute blast? I don't want to work for someone else for the rest of my life. You and me, all three of us, we're smarter now, more experienced, and we have some serious capital at our disposal. I know the tourism industry. You know international business. Deke, well, maybe he can build us a robotic cleaning system or something. But he can come to the annual shareholders' meetings. We'll have them in Hawaii, find you a hot girl, get you over your heartbreak."

"I'm not heartbroken." But Lex's words had him wondering if this might not be such a bad idea.

How amazing would it be to go into business with his two old friends? Lex and Deke were both brilliant. They were innovative and hard-working. Together, the three of them would have a real shot at building something successful.

He could throw all of his energy into the venture, totally focusing on business for the foreseeable future.

"Just how far have you thought this through?" he asked Lex.

"I just spent fourteen hours on airplanes. So, fourteen hours, plus a three-hour layover."

"Is the Sagittarius even for sale?"

"It will be," said Lex. "The family who owns it is having some…challenges. That's what kicked off my plan. Rita Loring just discovered her husband is sleeping with his assistant, putting the pre-nup in her favor. I know she'll sell her share. The woman couldn't care less about the hotel, and she'll get a kick out of ruining Lewis Loring. Her daughter will support her. If I offer, both women will sell their shares of the business and go on a shopping spree. And Lewis will be left with a choice between staying on as a minor shareholder and cashing out. Since the place has lost money the past three years in a row, I'm betting he'll cash out."

"How do you know all this?" Deke asked.

"I talk to people," said Lex. "I buy them drinks. Sometimes I sleep with them."

"You slept with Rita Loring?" Evan voiced the first thought that popped into his mind.

Lex's expression twisted into a grimace. "I slept with her daughter."

Deke coughed out a laugh. "I'm in."

"The daughter's not ticked off?" asked Evan.

"The daughter's already moved on. She's got bigger fish than me to reel in. It'll take me a week or two to put the deal together. But we've got to move fast."

Both men stared at Evan.

"I have to decide right now?" He glanced at the half-built shelves, thinking his evening plans had taken a huge left turn.

"Yes, you have to decide right now," Lex mocked. "What's to decide?"

It was a fair question. Of all of them, Evan was the guy in the best position to make a big change in his life. He had to make a change. The status quo had ceased being an option over a week ago.

His mind shifted to Angie. He told himself, really *truly*

told himself, that it was over. There was absolutely no going back. Forward was his only choice.

"Okay," he said, forming a plan in his mind as he spoke. "I've got some liquid investments and the cash from the Pasadena house. And J.D. left me several million dollars in his will. I was going to donate it to charity or maybe burn it in protest. But I suppose it's honorable to contribute it to the cause."

"You're in?" Lex asked with a grin.

"I'm in," Evan stated with conviction.

"We need a very old bottle of scotch," said Deke, fishing his car keys out of his pocket, "to toast our new venture."

Angelica had dressed in an ultrafeminine outfit once again in an effort to impress Conrad. But she needn't have bothered. He wasn't at home, and it was Albert, the butler, who showed her and Evan inside. They were meeting with the catering manager and the florist to tour the house and settle some questions about the setup and décor for the wedding.

Kayla and Matt had made it as far as Edinburgh on their way back home. They'd sent several texts while in the airport changing planes. They were thrilled with the wedding plans and reported that everything seemed set for the art exhibit. By now, they'd be over the Atlantic on their way to New York. Once they made it to California, the wedding planning was going to get a whole lot simpler for Angelica and Evan.

Albert, who seemed exceedingly good at his job, had offered her a glass of chardonnay this time instead of the single malt. Evan had chosen a beer.

The group worked their way through an impressive kitchen and dining area, agreeing that the bride should come down the grand staircase, and discussing how the great room should be set up for the ceremony. The guests could then mingle on the terrace and even on the beach at low tide, while staff replaced the folding chairs used for the ceremony and set up the tables for a sit-down dinner.

The caterer seemed impressed with the kitchen, and had requested extra prep tables in the breakfast room. The florist took pictures and measurements, and went over photos of the arrangements Kayla had already chosen, ensuring they would still work with the new décor. Soon they had what they needed.

While Albert showed the florist and caterer out, Angelica wandered across the terrace, trying to imagine Kayla's smile and her mother's delight at the amazing surroundings. She made her way to the lowest level of the terrace then gave in to temptation, taking the narrow staircase down to the beach level.

The tide was out, leaving a wide strip of damp sand exposed beyond the rocky shore. She kicked off her shoes to pick her way to the shore.

The sky was clear, and the half-moon illuminated an orange buoy about thirty yards out. She captured her hair in her hand, holding it against a gust of wind. Her aqua silk wraparound dress rustled against her legs. As she moved toward the water, she heard the sound of Evan's footfalls behind her.

"Reminds me of the opening scene in *Jaws*," she observed.

"Going skinny-dipping?"

"Not on your life."

"Chicken," he mocked softly.

"Uh-huh," she agreed, taking a sip of the crisp wine. "Do you think they'll be happy?"

"Matt and Kayla?"

"Yes. Not with each other. That's a given. I mean with the arrangements we're making. I know we've done our best, but it's hard to second-guess people." It was shaping up to be a wedding that Angelica would love. But what bride wanted someone else to do the planning for her?

"It was their decision to go to Scotland," said Evan. He was standing beside but slightly behind her as she gazed out at the dark water.

"They didn't expect the storm."

"Or the need for the extra approval."

"At least they got the exhibit." Kayla had come across as very excited in her texts to Angelica.

"It's all coming together for them." There was a wistful note in Evan's voice.

Angelica could relate to that emotion. When they'd first introduced Matt and Kayla to each other, she and Evan had been the stable couple, happy, in love and newly engaged. Back then, it had been Matt and Kayla helping with preparation for Angelica and Evan's wedding. A lump formed in her throat at the memories.

"You okay?" Evan asked.

"Fine," she lied, gathering her emotions. "How about you?"

"It's all good."

She forced herself to carry on with small talk. "Are you getting settled in Santa Monica?"

"I am."

"How's the business?" She knew leaving Lassiter Media had to have been a professional setback for him, and she truly wished him well.

"Deke and I might start working together. Lex, too."

She turned to him. "I thought you were going out on your own."

"I was planning on it. But we're looking at a possible deal that involves all three of us."

"What is it?"

"I'm not in a position to say."

Of course he wasn't. And even if he was, it was certainly none of her business. "I'm sorry. I didn't mean to pry."

"Everything going okay for you?" he asked.

"I'm moving my office. I didn't…" She stumbled a bit, realizing she was about to share the truth with him. "I mean, I couldn't…well, bring myself to take over Dad's office. So I'm converting the top floor boardroom into an office for me."

Evan was quiet for a moment. "That seems like a good idea, differentiating yourself for your father."

"That's my plan."

The sound of the waves filled in the silence between them.

"So, did Conrad really bring you an idea for a television series?" Evan asked.

"He's been in contact. He hasn't sent us anything yet, but it looks like he's serious."

"I thought he was just testing you."

"I did too. But he actually gave me an idea for a new direction for LBS."

"I'm glad you have some new ideas."

"I've always had ideas," she said defensively.

"I wasn't criticizing you, Angie."

She hated it when he used that nickname. Okay, she liked it when he used that nickname. But she hated that she liked it. It was endearing and intimate, strumming her memories. How many times had he said it while they'd made love?

I love you, Angie, he'd whisper in her ear. No matter how often he said the words, her breath would catch, and her heart would sing, and her world would settle into a perfect dome of contentment. Even now, she was fighting an urge to lean back against him.

"Angie?"

She shook herself and headed toward the waves, letting the cold water shock her to reality. She waded to her ankles, her knees, her thighs.

"Whoa," Evan caught her arm.

She shook him off.

"I thought we'd decided against skinny-dipping."

"I don't need your help." She didn't need it here or anywhere else.

"I honestly wasn't criticizing you. I have nothing but respect for your abilities at Lassiter Media."

"Is that why you fought so hard to keep me out?"

"Is that how you remember it?"

"I remember." She paused, gathering her thoughts as the waves pushed against her legs, washing the sand from beneath her feet. "I remember being abandoned by everyone I ever loved."

"Yeah?" There was a funny note to his voice. "How did that make you feel?"

The question struck her as absurd. "How do you think it made me feel? Terrible. I felt terrible."

There was a lengthy silence, and then his tone was hollow. "Do you know how many people in this world loved me?"

For some reason, each of his words felt like a punch to her stomach.

"You," he continued. "You were the only one, Angie. So, yeah, I know exactly how that makes a person feel."

Her chest contracted with pain. She turned, and a wave splashed up, dampening her dress.

"Evan…" She didn't know what to say. She knew his parents had died when he was a teenager, knew he had no brothers or sisters. Her family might be scattered and unorthodox, but it was definitely a family in every sense of the word.

"You were supposed to be my other half." He spoke softly into the night. "You were supposed to have my babies and turn this solitary existence into a big, rambunctious, loving family."

Her chest turned into one big ache, and tears threatened behind her eyes. Then a big wave pushed against her side. She staggered, then fell, gasping as the cold water engulfed her, the wave swirling over her head.

In a split second, his hand was on her arm, yanking her upright.

"What the hell?"

"I tripped," she sputtered.

He scooped the wineglass full of seawater from her hand. "Let's get out of here."

She trotted miserably toward the shore, his hand firmly on her upper arm, tugging her along. Her heart ached with regret. She'd made some terrible mistakes these past months. She'd been angry, disappointed and despondent.

But in all that time, with all those disputes and maneuvers, she'd never felt as heartsick as she did in this moment.

Angelica arrived at the Lassiter mansion still soaking wet. Albert had given her a fluffy, white robe to cover her ruined dress, and she'd combed out her hair and washed off the worst of her smudged makeup in Conrad's powder room. But she still looked like a drowned rat.

The last thing she needed was to find her two brothers waiting for her in the front foyer. She'd known they were both in town with their wives, but they'd fallen out of the habit of staying at the mansion.

"Explain this to us so that we understand," Dylan began, as they came to their feet.

"I fell in the ocean." She shut the door behind her. She was too tired for this, so she slipped past them into the study, helping herself to a brandy snifter and uncapping a bottle of cognac.

They both followed on her heels.

"We're talking about you and Evan," said Sage.

"That's a l—" She stopped herself mid-word.

She'd been about to confess that it was all a lie. But she knew that Evan was right. If she told her brothers the truth, she'd have to ask them to lie to their loved ones. She couldn't do that. But she also couldn't risk an accidental leak before Kayla's wedding.

"It's a long shot," she said instead, her back to them as she poured a measure of the cognac into the blown crystal glass.

"What the hell happened?" Dylan demanded. "One minute you can't even contemplate forgiveness, the next the newspaper has you reuniting."

"It's complicated," she said, turning to face them. "You'll have to leave it at that for now."

"I don't think so," said Dylan, advancing on her.

"We talked," said Angelica, looking her brother square in the eyes. "We reminisced." She inwardly winced as she recalled tonight's hurtful conversation. "We agreed that we'd both made some mistakes. And we've decided to spend a little time together."

There. Everything she'd just said was true. She took a sip of the cognac.

Sage moved to stand beside Dylan. "What aren't you telling us?"

"What I'm not telling you, is how this all ends. Because I don't know how it all ends."

They both peered at her with obvious suspicion.

"We were very much in love," she told them. "What we went through was painful and emotional. We're both battered and bruised, and we don't know where that leaves us."

Her brothers' gazes softened in sympathy.

She realized they were buying it.

She also realized that the reason they were buying it was because she was buying it. Because it was true. It was all so frighteningly true that she wanted to weep.

"Oh, Angie," Dylan sighed, drawing her into his arms.

She held her drink out to one side and accepted his hug.

"I wish I could explain better than that," she whispered.

"We understand that you can't," said Sage, giving her a rub on the arm. "We can wait."

She drew back, wishing she could be completely open with them. "Thank you. Thank you for being patient with me."

"You're freezing," said Dylan, tightening his hug and rubbing his hands up and down her back.

"I am. And I'm exhausted. I think I'm going to take a bath and go straight to bed."

"That's a good idea," said Sage. "Do you want me to get Colleen to come over?"

Angelica managed a smile. "I don't need a nurse. What I really need is a good night's sleep."

"Okay," Sage agreed.

Dylan plunked a kiss on her head. "Call us if you need anything."

She hiccupped out a laugh. "I'm not used to you guys being this way."

"I suppose not," Dylan agreed. "But I like it better when we're not fighting."

"So do I," said Angelica, battling a surge of guilt. She stepped away from Dylan, feeling as though she was accepting their affection under false pretenses. "Now, you two get out of here so I can warm up."

They both wished her good-night and headed down the hall to the front foyer and out the door.

Angelica sipped at the brandy as she made her way up the main staircase to her bedroom. She was chilled to her bones, aching and shivering uncontrollably as she stripped off her wet dress and clinging underwear, tossing them into the sink to rinse off the saltwater, wondering if there was anything she could do to save the patterned silk. Then she turned the taps in the oversized tub, and hot bathwater churned from the big faucet to fill it.

Leaving the dress to soak, she dumped some scented oil into the bathwater, lit a few candles, and then finally sank into the deep water. She laid her head back and let the warmth seep into her skin.

Evan's image immediately bloomed in her mind. His anger and disappointment hurt as much now as it had in those moments on the beach. She'd known all along that he wanted a big family. She'd wanted one, too. She'd also known he was alone in the world. But she'd never imagined him being lonely.

She felt a ridiculous urge to reach out to him, comfort him, help him somehow. But she knew there was nothing she could do. She'd made her choice five long months ago when she'd decided to mistrust him, to team up with Jack Reed and fight Evan for Lassiter Media. She reminded herself for what seemed like the hundredth time that there was absolutely nothing she could do to fix things now.

Five

As he and Deke made their way across the ten-story atrium lobby of the Sagittarius Resort, Evan considered the possibility that Deke could be right about the danger of spending time with Angie. Last night, when he'd pulled her dripping and vulnerable from the surf, protectiveness had welled up inside him. He'd wanted to hoist her into his arms and carry her off. He'd been forced to slam a lid on the urge before he could figure out where he'd carry her and what he'd do when he got there.

"Maybe we should spend a couple of days here incognito," Deke suggested. "Get rooms, check out the facilities, see how things are run."

Lex was looking into the company's financial records, while Evan and Deke were taking a more hands-on approach to investigating their potential purchase. So far, they'd toured the beach, the pool, the beachfront café and the gourmet restaurant on the top floor. Now, they were on their way to the eighteen-hole golf course.

Before Evan could decide on the usefulness of taking things undercover, Deke redirected his attention. "Look. There's the sports bar."

They altered their path, swerving to take in a couple thousand square feet of steel-gray leather, brick work and big screen TVs. The floor was worn wood, the bar top immaculate, and the pool tables in the back looked beautifully kept.

"What we should do," Evan suggested, "is hold Matt's bachelor party here. A round of golf, a game on the big screen, brews, burgers and a few pool matches. Then we can all book rooms and stay over. We'll poll everyone in the morning and see how they liked their stay."

Deke grinned. "Kill two birds with one stone? I like it. Maybe we can get Kayla and the bridesmaids to check out the spa."

Evan's brain wrapped itself around the thought of Angie in a spa, or anywhere else for that matter.

"I'm not interested in a hot stone massage," Deke continued. "Never mind a facial or some waxing."

Even shook off the image of Angie. "Ouch."

"Yeah. Ouch. I say we sacrifice the women."

"That kind of thinking is why you'll never have more than one-night stands."

"Who wants more than one-night stands?"

Evan's phone chimed in his pocket.

"Most guys over the age of twenty-one," he noted as he answered the familiar number. "Hey, Matt. You're on the ground?"

"Taxiing to the terminal at LAX," came Matt's reply.

"Welcome home."

"Thanks. It's been an adventure. You around tonight?"

While Evan talked, he and Deke exited the sports bar and began to make their way to the golf course. "Sure. Absolutely. Deke and I are just checking out a place for your bachelor party."

"Deke's in town?" asked Matt.

"He is."

"Can he stay for the wedding?"

"Hang on." Evan moved the phone away from his mouth. "Matt wants to know if you can come to the wedding."

"I already told Tiffany I'd be her date."

The information took Evan by surprise. "You did?"

"She asked. And I still haven't seen her naked."

"You watch yourself," Evan warned.

But Deke just laughed.

"He's coming with Tiffany," Evan told Matt.

"That's great." There was a muffled sound at Matt's end of the line. "Kayla wants to know when you and Angelica got back together."

Evan made a guess of what had happened. "She read the *Morning Break?*"

"She found it online while we were at JFK."

"We aren't back together," Evan corrected. "Yet."

"Well, get a move on, will you?"

"Sure. No problem. How do you feel about the Sagittarius Resort golf course and sports bar?"

"What for?"

"Your bachelor party."

"Sounds expensive. Who's paying?"

"Deke's paying."

Deke gave an unconcerned shrug.

"Then I leave it in your capable hands, best man." There were some pings in the background, followed by a voice over the airplane loudspeaker. "We're at the gate. I'll call you from the apartment. I think Kayla just set up the final tux and dress fittings at the his-and-hers wedding place for tonight."

"Text me the details."

"Will do. And, hey man, thanks for all your help this week."

"Happy to do it." Evan signed off.

Deke pushed open a glass door that led to a patio and the pro shop.

"I'm not crazy about this thing with Tiffany and the wedding," Evan felt compelled to state as they walked.

"Why not? She doesn't have a boyfriend, and I already know Matt and Kayla. It seemed like a pretty logical solution."

"But you're not dating her. You're only trying to sleep with her."

"Of course I'm trying to sleep with her. Have you looked at her?"

"She's Angie's friend, Deke."

"And you're Angie's ex. So you shouldn't even care. Besides, I haven't exactly kept my goal a secret. She knows perfectly well that I've got the hots for her."

"I hope you used those exact words."

Deke chuckled. "I did. She told me not to hold my breath."

They came to the edge of the patio, where clusters of dining tables overlooked the golf course. Evan braced his hands on the rail, letting the topic slide. Deke was right. Tiffany knew the score, and Evan knew Deke wouldn't push it if she said no.

As expected, the golf course was magnificent. Wide, emerald fairways followed the natural contours of the land. Palm trees swayed in the wind, while the overall layout sloped down to the cliff's edge, offering stunning views of the blue ocean.

"They host three professional tournaments a year," said Deke. "Plus top-flight amateur events. And their list of VIP members is impressive. I say we buy the place for the Rolodex alone."

Evan's phone chimed again.

Deke nodded toward the sound. "It's hard to believe you're currently unemployed."

"It's hard to believe your phone is staying so quiet."

Deke patted his shirt pocket. "I forwarded all the business

calls directly to Colby. You know, I'm beginning to think I don't actually have a personal life."

"You're a workaholic," Evan reminded him.

"True enough."

Evan didn't recognize the number, so he assumed it was a business call. "Hello?"

"Mr. McCain?"

"Yes."

"This is Geoff Wilson, *Los Angeles Star Daily*."

Uh oh.

"I'm doing a story on Lassiter Media, and I was wondering if you had any comment on the recent revelation that your engagement to Angelica Lassiter is back on?"

Evan knew he couldn't alienate the press without losing Conrad's support, so he didn't hang up. Instead, he chose his words carefully, hoping to drop enough breadcrumbs to keep the reporter happy. "My relationship with Ms. Lassiter is a private matter."

"She's pictured in the *Weekly Break* without an engagement ring."

"I haven't seen that *Weekly Break*."

"Does it surprise you that she's not wearing her engagement ring?"

"It does not." Evan covered the receiver with his hand, whispering to Deke. "Get Angelica on your phone." He needed to warn her about potential calls from reporters. And they needed to make sure they kept their stories straight.

Deke's brows went up, but he extracted his cell phone and dialed.

"So, you're saying there's no engagement?" asked Geoff Wilson.

"I'm saying it's a private matter."

"Where's the ring?"

Evan decided stalling was still the best way to go. "Ms. Lassiter and I would appreciate privacy while we—"

"Are the two of you back together or not?"

"Ms. Lassiter and I would appreciate privacy while we discuss our reconciliation."

"You do know this is L.A., right?"

Evan couldn't help but crack a smile. "The Lassiter family has been through a difficult time."

"How will you feel about playing second fiddle to your wife at Lassiter Media?"

"That's not an issue, since I'm no longer working at Lassiter Media."

Deke had turned away, and was talking in a low voice on his phone.

"Did she fire you?" the reporter asked.

Evan wished he could end the call, but he wanted to keep the press satisfied, and the last thing he needed was to ramp up the story any further. "I resigned from Lassiter Media. I'm now pursuing some independent business opportunities."

"Will you go back to Lassiter Media after you marry Angelica?"

"Lassiter Media is in very capable hands. Angelica Lassiter will make an excellent CEO. And I'm certain her father would be proud."

"Proud of the way she fought his will?"

Evan felt like he was navigating a mine field. "It was a complicated situation. But we're all focused on the future. And I'm afraid I have another pressing appointment right now. Do you have a final question?"

"Did you give her back her ring?"

Evan hesitated for a moment. "Can I go off the record?"

Geoff Wilson paused. Evan knew the man would hate to get a juicy scoop off the record, but he'd hate it more to miss a juicy scoop altogether.

"Sure," he finally answered. "Off the record."

"Not yet. But I am planning to give it back."

"When? Where?"

Evan chuckled. "If we decide we want our pictures in the paper, you'll be the first person we call. Goodbye, Mr. Wilson."

"But—"

Evan disconnected the call.

"Off the record?" asked Deke. "Are you kidding me?"

Evan took Deke's phone and pressed the microphone against his leg to block his voice. "I know it's a long shot that he'll respect it. But I had to give him something. And it would be worse if he printed his suspicions that we're not really getting back together."

Evan raised the phone to his ear. "Angie?"

"What's going on?" She sounded breathless.

"Are you okay?"

"Fine."

"Are you running from someone?"

"I'm on an exercise bike."

Evan struggled not to picture her in tight exercise pants and a cropped T-shirt. "I just had a call from a reporter. A guy from the *Los Angeles Star Daily*."

Her tone turned guarded. "What did he want?"

"To grill me about our relationship. You're going to the fitting tonight?"

"The bridesmaid dresses? Yes. Grill you how?"

"The usual. Are we back together? How do I feel about it? Am I working at Lassiter Media again? I'll pick you up, and we can go together tonight."

"I can get there myself."

"If the press is calling me, they're likely following you. We have to make this look good."

"Evan, I am not going to spend the next two weeks—"

"Yes, you are. You're going to spend the next two weeks pretending you like me."

"Evan."

"We're too far down the road to back off now. I'll pick you up at seven."

"I won't be home."

"Where will you be?"

She went silent, and he could feel her stubbornness right through the line.

"Fine," she huffed. "I'll be home."

"I'll see you at seven."

Kayla had a flare for the feminine and the beautiful, and everything about her custom-made wedding reflected her good taste. Her bridal gown was both traditional and spectacular. Made of pure, white satin, the wraparound bodice hugged her slim torso. A band of delicate jewels accentuated her bust, while the full skirt, with its cascading jeweled vine pattern, started at her hips and flowed to the floor where it flared out in a three-foot train.

"It's absolutely stunning," Angelica breathed, blown away by the picture Kayla made in the dressing area of the wedding store.

"You look like a fairy princess," said Tiffany, moving around for a look at the back.

"I was thinking hair up," said Kayla, demonstrating.

"Definitely," Angelica agreed. "Do you have a diamond necklace?"

"And dangling, diamond earrings," said Tiffany.

Angelica moved closer to check out the pattern of the jewels on the dress. "I've got the perfect thing," she told Kayla. "It's a four-row diamond choker." Then she wondered if she was being too presumptuous. "If you'd like something borrowed, I mean."

"I don't remember it," said Tiffany.

"I don't wear it very often. My brothers gave it to me for my nineteenth birthday. It's a little too dressy for most occasions."

"I'd love to borrow it," said Kayla. Then she took a step back, turning away from the mirror. "Now let me get a look at the two of you."

Angelica focused on the mirror, gazing at herself in an ice-pink, full-length bridesmaid gown. The tight, strapless, satin bodice glistened with silver sequins. It laced up the back, starting at the base of her spine and ending several inches below her shoulder blades in a sexy, low, V cut. An organza skirt, scattered with sequins, floated like a cloud around her ankles.

Given the time constraints, they were buying off the rack. But the store had a huge variety of styles to choose from.

"You both look perfect," said Kayla.

Tiffany twirled around. "I feel like dancing already."

"Matt says you're bringing Deke as your date," Kayla said.

"That's right. He's a fun guy and a really good dancer."

Tiffany stopped twirling, and the three women stood side by side in front of the mirror.

"You've been dancing with Deke?" Angelica asked, curious.

"Just that one night after dinner. Neither of us was tired. Nothing else happened."

"I assume you'd tell me if it did."

"Maybe." Tiffany grinned.

"I think it all works," said Kayla.

Angelica pulled her attention back to the mirror. She agreed with Kayla. The dresses looked exquisitely beautiful—a little girlie for her normal tastes, but definitely beautiful.

"Well, that was quick," said Tiffany.

"I'm nothing if not efficient," said Kayla.

Both of the other two women groaned at the joke. Kayla could shop until she dropped.

"So, is the thing with Deke serious?" Kayla asked Tiffany.

Angelica found herself wondering the same thing. She knew Tiffany was attracted to him, and the reverse was obviously also true. But she'd thought it was more of a flirtation than anything else. She had been surprised when Tiffany invited him to the wedding.

"He's hot," said Tiffany.

"That doesn't answer the question," Angelica noted.

"It's not serious," said Tiffany, but her glance moved away as she said it. "Can't a girl have a good time?"

"Of course you can," said Kayla, an apology in her tone. "We don't judge. You should have as many good times as you want."

"Okay, I didn't have *that* good a time."

"My point is that you can," said Kayla.

"I agree," Angelica said with conviction. "All flings don't have to be romantic."

A fleeting expression of guilt crossed Tiffany's face.

Before Angelica could consider what it meant, Kayla turned. "Can somebody unbutton me?"

As Angelica started unfastening the long row of tiny buttons, she couldn't help wonder if Tiffany was masking deeper feelings for Deke. Could she be worried about Angelica's reaction? Angelica didn't mind if the two of them dated. Just like she didn't mind that Kayla and Matt were a loving couple.

Her and Evan's friends had gotten together, while she and Evan had split apart. That was life. It was ironic that she and Evan had been the ones to introduce both couples, but it didn't change the fact that she wished them every happiness.

"You guys stay dressed up," said Kayla as she made her way into the changing room. "We can't let Matt see my dress, but I want to put you beside the groomsmen and see how you look."

"It's okay if you like him," Angelica told Tiffany as the curtain shut behind Kayla. "Don't hold back because of me."

"Who says I'm holding back?" Tiffany was silent for a moment, then said, "I saw that you drove here with Evan?"

It was Angelica's turn to feel a pang of guilt. She knew Tiffany had seen the *Weekly Break* article, but they hadn't had a chance to talk about it yet. She felt sick at the thought of lying again.

She swallowed, girding herself to tell the fake story. She couldn't look Tiffany in the eyes. "We're, uh, trying to spend a little time together. You know…to maybe see what happens."

"Angie."

"Yes." Angelica couldn't seem to bring her voice above a whisper.

"Deke told me."

"Deke told you what?"

"About the two of you tricking Conrad."

Angelica was speechless.

"I understand why you're doing it," Tiffany continued, "but I have to say, I'm not sure it's such a good idea."

"How did Deke figure it out?"

"Evan told him."

"But…" Anger formed in the pit of Angelica's stomach. She went hot, then cold, her tone a hiss. "We swore. We swore we weren't going to tell anyone. Not even my brothers."

"I won't tell anyone."

"I trust *you*. It's Evan who betrayed me. I can't believe he did that. I *lied* to my own brothers."

"You're mad at him. That's a good thing for your psyche. Hold on to it."

Kayla pulled back the change room curtain with a clatter. "What are you guys doing for shoes?"

"We should match them," said Tiffany, easily changing topics and looking down at her feet.

Angelica forcibly pushed aside her frustration and anger. She didn't want her problems to impact on Kayla's happiness.

"You think white?" she asked, in the calmest voice she could muster. She glanced down at the western boots she'd put on with her jeans this morning. "Or silver? Silver's probably better. Open toed or closed."

"Should we shop?" asked Kayla.

"I'm up for it," Angelica agreed.

"Heck yeah," said Tiffany. "You're the bride. We'll do whatever you want."

Kayla grinned. "This is fun. What else can I get in the next two weeks?"

"Anything you want," said Angelica. "Just name it."

"I want a spa day."

"I'm definitely in on that," said Tiffany.

"Apparently the guys are doing golf and a kegger."

An entire day at the spa sounded like a very big time commitment to Angelica. But she reminded herself she was striving for work-life balance. She'd figure out a way to swing it. It would take a few extra late nights, but she'd make up the time.

"Let's do it," Angelica said with conviction.

"It's a date," said Kayla. "Now, let's go see how the guys look." She ushered Angelica and Tiffany toward the doorway.

Leaving the dress shop, they passed through a storefront full of flowers, stemware and satin accessories, then passed under an archway to the tux fitting area.

Though there were several men in the room, Angelica's gaze immediately zeroed in on Evan. There was no word for him but magnificent. Standing in front of a triple mirror, he wore a classic black tuxedo, with a black vest and a white shirt. His tie was silver, with a subtle stripe of ice pink. The other groomsman, Silas, was wearing an identical outfit, while Matt had differentiated his outfit with a silver vest and a plain, black tie.

"Go stand beside them." Kayla sounded excited. "Matt, get out of the way."

"Are you turning into bridezilla?" Matt joked, stepping aside.

"Tiffany says I have two weeks to get everything all my own way."

Evan's gaze came to rest on Angelica, sweeping from her head to her toes and back again. It left a trail of heat in its wake.

Tiffany gave Angelica a subtle nudge, reminding her she was supposed to go stand next to Evan. She took a deep breath and forced her feet to move.

His gaze stayed on her as she approached. The warmth in his eyes was unmistakable. But she reminded herself she was angry with him. He'd told Deke their secret, after swearing he wouldn't.

"Nice dress," he offered in an intimate tone.

"Nice tux," she returned a little more crisply.

"Shall we?" He gestured to the big mirror.

Girding herself, she turned.

Her breath immediately caught in her throat. She knew it was the clothing, but they looked like the perfect couple. For a long moment, she was certain, someplace deep down in her soul, that they belonged together.

She frantically shook off the feeling.

"I'll be taller." She came up on her toes, trying to do something, anything, to erase the perfect picture. "I'll have higher shoes."

"I'll still have you beat," he pointed out. He was right. Her height was far from being a match for his.

"It works," Kayla called out from behind them. "You guys look terrific together. Everybody strike a dance pose."

Angelica dropped her heels back down to the floor, and shifted sideways. The last thing she wanted to do was hug Evan. But he slipped an arm around her waist, using the momentum to turn her around, and pull her snug against his shoulder.

"Act natural," he whispered against her ear. "Remember, they think we're back together."

She found her voice. "Deke doesn't." A welcome wall of anger went up around her feelings. "You told Deke."

"Smile," said Evan.

"I lied to my brothers, and you went and told Deke."

"Can we not talk about this right now?" He took her hand in his and struck a dance pose.

"He told Tiffany. So now she knows."

Evan snuggled her to his body, and a rush of desire flooded her skin. "Later."

"Why did you tell Deke?"

"Because it was more dangerous to keep him in the dark."

"You want me to trust you, yet—"

"I wanted you to trust me five months ago. You didn't."

"And it turns out I was right."

"Angie? Is everything okay?" Kayla's tone was searching.

Angelica quickly planted a smile on her face. "It's perfect. I love the dress. Evan is just arguing with me about shoes."

"What's to argue?" Kayla asked. "We haven't even bought them yet."

"He's afraid the heels will be too high," said Angelica. "And he'll look short."

"He can always come shopping with us," Kayla offered.

"Great idea," said Angelica. "Let's take Evan shoe-shopping."

"I'm afraid I'm busy," said Evan, while Matt and Silas laughed at him.

"We can reschedule, so that you can come along," Kayla offered sweetly.

"No need," said Evan. "Whatever the bride wants will be perfectly fine with me."

"That's the spirit," said Matt.

"What the bride wants is for everyone to be happy," said Kayla. "So, no more arguing."

"Yes, ma'am," said Evan. "I'll do everything in my power to keep Angie's temper in check."

"Excuse me?" Angelica retorted. "You're suggesting *I'm* the problem?"

"There is no problem, sweetheart," said Evan. Then he dropped a kiss on her mouth.

Through the roar of her body's reaction, she heard Kayla say, "It's so great to see you two back together again."

Angelica knew she had to put some distance between her and Evan. A minivan had followed them home from the dress fitting last night. It didn't take a rocket scientist to figure out it had been a reporter.

Since the Lassiter mansion was partially visible from the gates, Evan had made a show of walking her to the front door. He'd suggested coming inside to make it look good, but she'd flatly refused, prompting him to give her a lingering good-night kiss. She'd almost kissed him back. She'd come within a split second of giving in when he finally broke away.

Afterward, she'd lain awake half the night in frustration. When she finally fell asleep in the early morning hours, she dreamed of making love to him. She knew she had to get away.

It took her half the day to come up with a viable excuse to get out of L.A. But then Noah Moore, the vice president of LBS family programming at the Lassiter Media offices in Cheyenne handed it to her on a silver platter.

While Evan had been in charge of Lassiter Media, he'd bought up the licensing of several stations in Britain and Australia. Then this morning, Angelica had reviewed the drama series proposal from Conrad Norville. It was an undeniably exciting show idea, targeted to LBS.

She was impressed with Conrad's work, and made a quick

decision to commission a first season. Once she got past the mental roadblock of only using original programming developed in-house on LBS, she realized Lassiter could make an American version of the top-rated shows from the new British and Australian affiliates.

But Noah Moore hated the idea. Which meant Angelica needed to bring him on side. And it made sense for her do that in person. Normally, she'd have asked him to fly to L.A. But right now, she was jumping at the excuse to get out of the city for a couple of days.

At Van Nuys Airport, she went out onto the tarmac and mounted the steps to the Lassiter Media corporate jet. The plane comfortably sat twelve, but it would only be Angelica today, since she didn't see any need to drag her assistant along.

She'd meet with the managers who worked from the Lassiter offices in Cheyenne, convince Noah Moore of the merit of her plans, then spend some time at Big Blue. There was no place better than Big Blue with its rustic beauty for her to rest and regroup. There wouldn't be a single tabloid reporter for hundreds of miles.

The jet pilot greeted her at the door. "Welcome aboard, Ms. Lassiter."

She gave the fiftyish man a smile. "Hello, Captain Sheridan."

"Looks like a smooth flight tonight." He stepped back so that she could easily enter the aircraft. "They're calling for a bit of turbulence over the Rockies, but I think we can avoid it if we take a higher altitude."

"That's great to hear, Cap—" As she turned into the body of the aircraft, she stumbled to a halt. "What are *you* doing here?"

"Is something wrong?" asked Captain Sheridan from behind her.

"Going to Cheyenne," Evan answered with a lazy grin.

He was sitting in the second row, wearing blue jeans and a tan T-shirt, an ankle propped up on the opposite knee. A half-full bottle of beer sat on the table in front of him.

"Who invited *you*?"

"Chance," said Evan.

"Ms. Lassiter?" the captain asked.

She turned back. "Evan is not coming with us."

"I don't understand. Mr. Lassiter advised us that we would have—"

"Hey, Angie." Tiffany came into view behind the captain.

"Tiff?" Angelica reached out to steady herself on the back of a white leather seat. "Is something wrong?"

Tiffany grinned. "Everything's great."

"Four passengers tonight," the captain finished.

Deke appeared behind Tiffany. "Good evening, Captain." He shook the man's hand. "I've never seen Big Blue," he told Angelica. "I can't wait."

"Stop," Angelica shouted.

Everyone went silent.

"What's going on here?"

Evan rolled to his feet, moving close to her, lowering his voice. "We're going to Cheyenne."

"No, *we're* not. *I'm* going to Cheyenne."

"And the rest of us will keep you company."

"Is this a joke?"

"No, it's a con. Remember?" He tipped his head toward the back of the plane. "Let's talk in private."

Angelica quickly skimmed through her options. She could stamp her foot and kick them off the aircraft. She could leave herself, refusing to go on the trip. Or she could give in and let Evan get his way.

None of the options appealed to her.

"We're ready to go, Sheridan," Evan told the captain.

Angelica opened her mouth to protest. Evan wasn't the

CEO any longer. This was her airplane. The captain was her employee.

"Very good, sir," Captain Sheridan replied.

Tiffany had flown on the jet in the past, and she helped herself to a mini bottle of wine from the cooler.

"You thirsty?" she asked Deke.

Evan snagged his beer and began backing away toward the rear of the plane.

"Come on," he told Angelica. "I need to talk to you."

"I'll take a beer," said Deke. "Are those cashews?"

"I can't believe you're pulling this stunt," said Angelica. He was ruining her entire plan. The only reason she was flying to Cheyenne was to get away from him.

He took another backward step. "I can't believe you're running away."

She gave up and followed him. "I'm not running away. Because you're coming with me. And you're the thing I'm running from. So, why are you here?"

"Piece of advice, Angie. Don't ever try to make your living as a con artist. The question on everyone's mind is, are they reconciling or not? How's it going to look to someone like Conrad if you take off without me?"

"Like I have a job."

"It looks better if we're together."

"I don't want to be together."

There was an edge to his tone as he gestured to the seat in the last row. "Tough break. This isn't all about you."

"I never said it was."

The jet engines whined as the pilot poured on power, and she quickly took her seat.

"It's about Matt and Kayla," said Evan as he belted into the seat across the narrow aisle.

"I'm aware of that," she answered tartly.

The jet began to taxi.

"And we're all doing things we'd rather not."

Something in his tone send a jolt through her brain. It was suddenly crystal-clear that he didn't want to be with her either. The situation was as inconvenient and frustrating for him as it was for her. Difference was, he was taking it in stride, while she was complaining like a little girl.

What was wrong with her? Hadn't she learned anything from her father's will? It truly wasn't all about her. She had to pitch in and serve the collective good instead of being so focused on herself.

"I'm sorry," she said to Evan.

His jaw dropped open just as the jet rushed to full power, pushing them back in their seats as it accelerated along the runway.

"Excuse me?" Evan asked above the noise.

"You're right, and I'm wrong. Everybody's inconvenienced by this. You, me, Tiffany, Deke. But it's about Kayla and Matt, and I need to shut up and get on with it. The house at Big Blue is huge. I'll try to stay out of your way."

The jet lifted off the runway, climbing into the setting sun.

He studied her in silence for a long moment. "You surprise me."

She wanted to move on. "Why did you bring Tiffany and Deke?"

"I thought you'd be more comfortable with chaperones."

She nodded. "I am. It was nice of them to come."

"Deke's never seen Big Blue. He's curious."

Angelica found herself smiling, and some of the tension eased from her stomach at the thought of spending some time on the family ranch. "It's a fantastic place."

"It is," Evan agreed, his posture relaxing. "So, something going on in the Cheyenne office?"

"I need to talk to Noah Moore. He disagrees with a direction I want to take for LBS."

"That's what happens when smart people work together. You get different ideas."

"You still think I'm smart?" The question was out before she thought through the wisdom of asking.

"You're brilliant, Angie. That's never been the problem."

"I'd ask what the problem was, but I'm pretty sure I know the answer."

"You're fanatical, controlling and way too myopic."

"I didn't ask."

"That one was for free."

She leaned her head back on the soft headrest, staying silent as the flight leveled out. She drew a deep breath. "I am working on those flaws."

His voice was low and slightly cautious beside her. "Okay, now you're just freaking me out."

"I know I'm not perfect, Evan."

He didn't respond for a moment. "At the risk of bursting this Zen-Angie bubble thing you've got going, I have something to ask you. And it's probably going to make you mad."

Angelica didn't particularly like the sound of that. But she promised herself to try to take it in stride. "Ask away."

"I think you should wear your engagement ring for a while."

She turned to gape at him.

"It'll convince everyone we're serious."

Her mind galloped to catch up to his words. "You still *have* my engagement ring?"

"Of course I still have your engagement ring."

"I don't understand. Why would you keep it?"

"What would I do with it?"

"Return it. Get your money back."

He shook his head. "It's custom-made. And it's been in dozens of photographs. In the middle of the press frenzy, did you really want the Angelica Lassiter engagement ring to show up for sale on-line?"

"I never thought of that," she admitted.

"Yeah, well, you were a bit distracted."

"Thank you," she found herself saying. "Even when you hated me, you were thoughtful."

"I never hated you, Angie. I admit, I was mad as hell."

"So was I."

A beat went by. Then he reached into his pocket and produced a small, black leather box.

Everything inside Angelica stilled. Her chest went tight with intense anxiety. She gazed down at the familiar solitaire. She'd always loved the way the stylized band winked with tiny white and blue diamonds. It was traditional, with a twist. That was how she'd always thought of her relationship with Evan. It had all the elements of a typical romance, but then there was the added spice of their energetic lives. At one time, it was enhanced by their mutual love of Lassiter Media with all its facets and foibles. But that was gone.

"Angie?" he prompted.

She moved her gaze from the ring to him. "It would be difficult," she told him honestly.

"I know. But the press is outright asking why you're not wearing it. And I'm more convinced than ever that Conrad is calling our bluff."

"You think he knows we're faking?"

"I think he suspects. And it's occurred to me that he might use it as an excuse to mess up the wedding."

Angelica knew this wasn't about her, and she knew she had to be tough. But when she reached for the box, her fingers trembled.

"Go get me a really big glass of wine," she told Evan, determinedly taking the box from his hand. "And I'll put it on."

He seemed to hesitate for a moment. "Sure. Okay. No problem." He unclipped his belt and rose from his seat.

Angelica stared at the beautiful ring, imagined the cool, smooth platinum settling on her finger, the weight of the big diamond, the wink of the band whenever her hand moved across her peripheral vision.

"You okay?" came Tiffany's soft voice.

"Not really." Angelica looked up. "Did you know he was going to do this?"

Tiffany shook her head. "Though it makes sense."

"Never occurred to me in a million years," Angelica admitted. "I guess I thought Conrad would keep it to himself. Then I thought we'd tell a few friends, and everybody would give us space while we pretended to think about getting back together. But now… How am I going to do this?"

"You don't have to wear it."

"Yeah, I do."

Kayla's happiness was at stake. Evan was keeping up his end of the deal. Angelica had to step up as well.

She determinedly tugged the ring out of the display slot. Then, without giving herself time to think, she shoved it onto her finger.

"It doesn't burn or anything," she joked to Tiffany.

"That's encouraging," came Evan's voice as he returned with a glass of red wine.

"Hand it over," said Angelica, waving him forward. "And keep 'em coming."

Six

Evan had always loved the Big Blue ranch. It was symbolic of J.D. and the entire Lassiter family. It could be harsh and unpredictable, but it was self-sufficient and endlessly resilient. It stood like a sentinel, protecting those who sought its refuge.

It was good that Angie had come here. Despite their differences, he knew this was hard for her. He had to admit he was baffled by her attitude on the airplane. He couldn't quite get past the shock that she'd agreed to wear her engagement ring. And, unsettlingly, he couldn't quite shake the idea that she might have truly changed these past months.

"Angie," Marlene greeted her niece with open arms as the four trooped into the great room.

Though Marlene was Angie's aunt, she had been more of a mother figure, since Angie's own mother had passed away when she was just a baby. The older woman enfolded Angie in a warm embrace.

When Marlene pulled back, her attention turned to Evan. "It's *so* wonderful to have you back," she beamed, moving to give him a hug as well.

"Wonderful to see you, Marlene."

Marlene then glanced curiously at Tiffany and Deke.

Angie stepped in. "You remember my friend Tiffany? And this is Evan's friend Deke. Tiffany is also going to be a bridesmaid at Kayla's wedding."

"Welcome to Big Blue," Marlene offered warmly, leading the way into the great room.

She chatted with them there for a few minutes but soon apologized for being tired and retired to her own wing in the huge house.

Angie offered everyone a snack then dispensed guest-room assignments, putting Deke and Tiffany on the second floor near her own bedroom, while relegating Evan to one of the first-floor bedrooms behind the kitchen. He supposed he should be grateful she hadn't put him in the bunkhouse.

He wasn't tired, so when the others went upstairs he made his way outside to the huge, flagstone patio. The ranch stretched out around him for miles, a patchwork of groves and lush paddocks. It was peaceful now; the equipment was all shut down for the night and the animals were quiet. The big sky arched above him, scattered with bright stars and a crescent moon.

He sat down on one of the padded deck chairs facing away from the house, drinking in the fresh air and absorbing the ambiance.

"Not much like L.A.," said Deke, as he approached from the house. "Or Chicago for that matter."

"I like it," said Evan. "Oh, maybe not full-time like Chance does. But it's a great place to come to get your head on straight."

"Your head's not on straight?"

"Getting more crooked by the minute," Evan admitted.

"I tried to talk you out of this," Deke reminded him, swinging into the chair beside him.

"You try to talk me out of a lot of things."

"Sometimes I'm right."

"You're always right. I just don't often care."

Deke chuckled. "If things work out well with the Sagittarius, maybe we should buy a dude ranch next. That way, you can work on your head on a regular basis."

"It's usually not a problem. So, why aren't you upstairs finding an excuse to bother Tiffany?"

"She's with Angelica right now. But the night is young."

"You really think you have a shot?"

Deke shrugged. "I think she can see right through my usual charm."

"Has that ever happened before?"

"Not in recent memory. But I'm up for the challenge. So, how come you're not warning me off her anymore?"

"Because I know she's got your number."

Deke tapped his fingertips against the wooden arm of the chair. "Sad, but true. So, what's up for tomorrow? Are we going to ride horses, wrangle cows? Maybe drive a tractor?"

"Do you know how to ride a horse?"

"I do not."

"Angie's going into the office in Cheyenne."

"Are you going to follow her?"

"I wish I could. She said she was in a disagreement with one of the executives. Noah Moore. I'd like to know what it's about. Noah can be opinionated, but he knows his job. He's got a lot to offer the company."

"You don't work there anymore."

"I know that."

"Any chance I can talk you out of all this?"

Evan shot him an arched look. "I haven't decided to do anything yet."

"Sure you have. The woman's got your ring back on her finger."

"It's a ruse."

"Keep telling yourself that." Deke brought his hands down on the chair arms and propelled himself to a standing position. "I'm going to check things out upstairs."

"Good luck," Evan offered automatically.

"Right back at you, buddy." Deke clapped him on the shoulder before he walked away.

Evan settled back into the deep chair, letting his focus go soft on the stars that glowed on the horizon. Deke knew he was still attracted to Angie. No bombshell there. He'd be attracted to her until the day he died. But that didn't mean there was anything more to the engagement ring than a convenient distraction for Conrad and the press.

A ring in and of itself didn't mean a damn thing. It was the emotion behind it that counted. It was love, honesty and respect between two people that made an engagement ring, a wedding dress, even a couple's wedding vows have meaning. Without those things, the ring was just a piece of stone.

"I didn't see you there." Angie's voice interrupted his thought. "I'm sorry, I'll just—"

"Don't be silly. It's your house. I can move to somewhere—"

"You don't have to leave on my account."

"I'll stay if you'll stay," he offered. "It's not a bad idea, you know. For us to practice talking to each other."

"You think we need practice?"

"I think we're a little stilted right now."

"Fair enough." She sat down in the chair vacated by Deke.

He took note of her glass of wine. "Anaesthetizing yourself against the ring?" He was a little surprised she still had it on.

She covered the diamond with her thumb. "I should have offered you something. Are you thirsty?"

"I'm fine. You don't have to treat me like a guest." Then he realized the way that might sound. "Not to say I'm family. I meant that I know I'm an interloper. You can feel free to ignore me."

She took a contemplative sip of the wine. "You know, that's not the dumbest thing you've ever said."

"Thank you." He paused. "Just out of curiosity, what was the dumbest thing I ever said?"

She thought about that for a moment. "It was at the Point Seven sailing regatta the day we met. On the dock next to J.D.'s yacht, Purshing's Pride. You said: 'Hello, Angelica. I'm Evan McCain. I work for your father.'"

"You remember the moment we met?"

"You don't?"

"You were wearing navy slacks and a white cotton blouse. It had dark blue buttons, and I could just barely see your lacy bra underneath."

"You were checking out my bra?"

"I was checking out your breasts."

The light was dim on the patio, but he was pretty sure he'd made her blush.

"A gentleman would be ashamed of himself," she stated.

"A gentleman might not have said it out loud, but he'd be doing exactly the same thing."

"You're lucky my father never knew."

"Your father planned it all along."

"He did," she agreed. "He might be shrewd, but he's not subtle." She went quiet. "Why do you think he did it?"

"Which part?"

"Us. You and me."

"You and me is a lot of real estate, Angie."

She nodded then took another sip. "We've never talked about it, you know. His will, the grand scheme, what it did to us."

"We've shouted about it," said Evan.

"I guess we have." Her thumb was stroking over her engagement ring. She had beautiful hands, beautiful arms, beautiful shoulders.

He watched the diamond wink in the starlight, his emotions moving to the surface even as he tried to ground himself in reality. "I'm not sure there's anything more to say."

She lifted her gaze to his. "It would be nice if there was. It would be nice if there was a conversation that would get us from A to B in a way we'd understand and accept, so that we could move forward."

He gave in to temptation and took her left hand, holding it up so that he could gaze at the ring. "I'm only looking as far as the next two weeks."

"Understandable." She rose.

He stood with her. "Can you see past that?"

"I have to see past that. The January replacements are already underway."

"Always business with you."

Her voice was a whisper, but the hurt was clear. "That's not fair."

"Isn't it?" He drank in her beauty.

"I'm doing everything I can to help Kayla."

He couldn't stop himself. He had to touch her. He ran his index finger along the curve of her chin.

His voice was guttural. "While I'm doing everything I can to save myself."

She didn't bolt, and he stroked his spread fingers into her hair. Then he leaned down to mesh his lips to hers, letting the power of his longing obliterate all good sense.

Angelica knew that the last thing in the world she should be doing right now was kissing Evan. But she didn't stop. She couldn't stop.

His lips were tender, firm, hot against her own. He knew just when to apply pressure and when to back off. His tongue flicked out, setting off a spiral of sensation through her body, drawing a moan from deep in her chest. She stepped in, pressing full length against him, blindly setting her wineglass on a side table.

His free arm went around her waist and he pulled her close, kissing her deeply. Then he moved to the corners of her mouth, across her cheek, down her neck, easing open the collar of her shirt.

"We can't do this," she murmured, more to herself than to him.

"We won't," he breathed. "We never do."

His words didn't make sense. "We don't?"

He popped a button on her shirt. "I always wake up far too soon."

"Oh. Okay." She'd dreamed about him too. She didn't always wake up too soon, but she wasn't about to admit that he'd satisfied her many times in her sleep.

He popped another button. His lips were warm, the autumn breeze cool on her skin.

She ran her fingers through his short hair, inhaled his familiar scent, closed her eyes and let herself revel in the cocoon of Evan. Her free hand went to his shoulder, sliding over his bicep, and she was reminded of his strength. She kissed his chest through his T-shirt, fighting an urge to tear it off. She wanted to taste his skin.

Before she knew it, her shirt was open. He slipped his hands beneath, moving them to her bare back. She felt her nipples tighten against her bra, and she pressed her breasts to his warm, broad chest.

His voice was strained. "This feels so damn right."

"I know." Her hands had moved to the waist of his jeans. She was pulling his T-shirt free, reaching beneath it to stroke his bare skin.

He swore under his breath. Then his hand fisted around the hem of her blouse. He took a step backward, tugging her along. She stepped forward. Then she took another step, knowing where they were going. They'd been there before, made love there before, in a secluded alcove at the edge of the patio, screened by a rose-covered trellis.

She dared to look into his eyes. They were dark and intense, smoldering coffee. She knew she should tell him no.

One of them had to put a stop to this, and Evan looked like he was past the point of reason.

But her vocal cords weren't working. His intense gaze trapped her own, and she felt her pulse rate jump. Her skin was flushed with arousal, itching against her tailored blouse and straight skirt.

The light dimmed around them. As he backed up against the log wall, the momentum propelled her forward, and she braced her hands on his shoulders, coming flush against his body. He instantly kissed her. His lips were hotter than before, more intense, his tongue probing deeper.

This was such a terribly bad idea.

But his hands were on the clasp of her bra. And then it was free, and he pushed the shirt and bra from her shoulders. His hand closed over her breast, and she moaned against his lips. He stroked her nipple with his thumb, making her knees go weak.

"I've missed you," he rasped, even as his hand stroked over her rear, coming to the hem of her skirt before reversing to slide upward.

"Evan," she managed.

She didn't know what else to say. She could stop him with a word, but she'd missed him so much. She'd missed his kiss, his touch, his voice and his scent.

His fingertips grazed her panties, and passion surged within her. She couldn't wait another second.

"Now," she whimpered. "Oh, please, now."

He'd heard the words before, and he jerked to action. He stripped off her panties, still kissing her deeply. He loosened his jeans. Then he lifted her, turning to brace her against the wall.

He was inside her in seconds, and she nearly wept with relief. The sensation was so familiar, so satisfying and so intensely arousing. He moved, and she pressed her face to the crook of his neck. Her hands clasped his back, fisting into the fabric of his T-shirt.

His breathing was heavy. He'd broken out in a sweat. He knew just when to slow down and just when to speed up. His fingertips teased, while his lips left moist circles on her neck and shoulders.

All she could do was hang on tight, while her world tilted over the horizon, and color and sound hazed her brain.

"Evan," she cried, and his hand closed over her mouth. She cried out again, but the sound was muffled.

"Angie," he whispered in her ear. "Angie, Angie, Angie."

Her body contracted, and her arms convulsed. Evan groaned, holding her tight, kissing her hard, his body shuddering and then going still.

After long minutes, she blinked her eyes open to see the stars, the black outline of the barn, the glow of the deck lights filtering through the rose bush. It was the intensely familiar sight of Big Blue. Reality was all around her, and she was practically naked in Evan's arms.

"Uh oh," she muttered.

"I know we shouldn't have done that."

She drew back to look at him, her body still joined with his. "Can you think of a single dignified move I can make here?"

"I can't," he admitted.

"This is mortifying."

"Yeah. Okay. Well, maybe in a minute I'll work my way up to mortified. Right now I'm still feeling pretty satisfied."

She bopped him in the shoulder. "Well, stop."

"I'll try."

"Evan, we just had sex."

"No kidding."

"We *can't* do that."

"Turns out, we can."

"Will you please be serious?"

"I am being serious. I'll be appalled in a minute. But right now, well…" He glanced at her bare breasts. "I want to memorize the moment."

"You have to forget all about this moment." She was going to find a way to do exactly that.

"Okay," he agreed.

"I mean it, Evan. We have to forget this ever happened."

"I will."

But then he kissed her, and she automatically kissed him back. It was tender and sweet, and it felt like goodbye.

"I'm sorry, Angie," he whispered as he eased them apart.

He set her gently on the ground, smoothing her skirt and adjusting his jeans. Then he stepped away to pick up her blouse and bra.

In the few seconds it took him, she struggled to regroup. It had been a slipup, for sure. But now that they'd done it, now that the urge was out of her system, perhaps things would get easier.

"You're going to the office in the morning?" he asked handing her the clothes.

"Yes." She shrugged into the lacy white bra, trying to forget that he was watching.

"You want some help?"

She felt a flash of annoyance. "I don't need your help."

"I got to know Noah pretty well over the past few months."

Having her shirt back on gave her confidence. "I can handle Noah."

"I'm not saying you can't. They're going to see your ring."

She reflexively glanced at her left hand, fighting a surge of emotion that came along with the sight of the diamond.

"They'll think I'm back in the game," Evan continued. "It wouldn't be so strange for me to show up with you."

"I'll tell them you're not working for Lassiter Media. We're not pretending that," she warned. "Not even temporarily."

"I agree."

"That's a first."

He took a step closer. "Hey, I agreed we shouldn't make love."

"Fat lot of good that did me."

He flexed a grin. "What is it you and Noah disagree on?"

"None of your business."

"I'm trying to help."

"Don't."

"Seriously, Angie. Is there some kind of trouble?"

"No trouble, Evan. None at all." Well, except for the fact that she'd just had sex with her ex-fiancé. That was definitely trouble.

She refastened the last button then met his eyes. She didn't have the faintest idea what to say in this situation. Simple seemed best.

"Goodnight, Evan."

"Goodnight, Angie."

She moved past him.

"Sleep well," he called from behind.

She didn't acknowledge his words. Instead, she retrieved her wineglass on the way across the patio and headed for the staircase to her bedroom. She *would* sleep well, she told herself. For a few hours at least, she was going to forget about everything complicated in her life.

Tomorrow would come soon enough. Tomorrow, she'd compound her lies by wearing Evan's ring in public.

Evan left Deke and Tiffany to a morning horseback ride under the capable care of a Big Blue ranch hand, while he headed into town. Angie's decision to fly to the Cheyenne office had been unexpected and abrupt. Evan wasn't a fool. If something wasn't seriously wrong, she would have waited until after the wedding.

He still had plenty of people he could trust at Lassiter

Media. He was going to sleuth around, see what he could find out. There were a lot of nuances and complexities to the expansion he'd managed while he was CEO. He hadn't explained them to anyone, because he was ticked off when he left. But he didn't want Angie walking into a hornet's nest.

He parked the borrowed ranch pickup truck in the historic district, pocketing the keys in his blue jeans as he headed for the reception area of the red brick, six-story Lassiter Media building. In contrast to the exterior, the inside of Lassiter Media looked like it belonged in L.A., with chrome and glass, plenty of light and television screens showing the fare of the various Lassiter Media networks.

"Evan." The receptionist greeted him with a wide smile.

Clarissa was in her mid-thirties, friendly and down to earth, and she had a knack for keeping the entire building organized. If Evan had stayed, he'd have made her his personal assistant in the Cheyenne office.

"Morning, Clarissa," he offered as he approached the high counter.

"Are you looking for Angelica?" Clarissa gave him a wink. "I saw the rock was back on her finger."

"It is," Evan acknowledged. "But, no. I'm sure she has everything under control in the boardroom. I was wondering if Max was around."

Clarissa picked up her phone and punched a few buttons. "He should be in his office. But if he's not, I can page him. Will you be in town long?"

"Just a few days." It was a guess on his part.

"Max?" she said into the receiver. "Evan's here to see you." She paused and a smile grew on her face. "Yes, that Evan. You didn't see Angelica? The wedding's back on."

Evan kept a smile pasted on his face, knowing there'd be no stopping the gossip mill now. Next thing, there'd be speculation on a new wedding date.

"I know," said Clarissa, nodding at whatever Max had said. "You want to go on up?" she asked Evan.

"I was thinking we'd step out for a coffee."

"Can you come down?" she asked Max. "He wants to do coffee." She paused again. "Okay." Then she hung up the phone.

"He's coming right down. We've missed you, boss."

"I've missed you too."

"Any chance you'll come back?"

Evan shook his head. "That's not in the cards. I'm working with a couple of old friends on some deals in L.A."

"But you'll visit Cheyenne. You'll come to town when Angelica does."

"I hope so."

"When's the wedding? It'll be at Big Blue, right? I'm dusting off my dress and rewrapping the gift."

Evan wished he could tell her to return the gift. He hoped she hadn't spent much on it.

The elevator door whooshed open, and Max Truger appeared. Barely into his thirties, he was director of integrated content at LBS, but he generally had his finger on the pulse of Noah's priorities in family programming.

"Welcome back," Max said, reaching out to shake Evan's hand.

"I'm not back. Not at Lassiter, anyway. Have time for coffee?"

"You bet." Max turned to Clarissa. "Can you bump my ten o'clock?"

"Sure thing."

"I don't want to mess up your day," said Evan.

"It's an internal meeting. No problem." Max turned for the door. "The Shorthorn Grill?"

"Sounds good." Evan would enjoy the walk.

They exited through the wide front door, onto a sidewalk lined with well-preserved, historic buildings. The mid-morning traffic was light, but several pickup trucks sped by, along with a shiny, vintage red Cadillac that belonged to a famous local rancher.

"So, what's going on?" asked Max, watching Evan with an astute expression. The two had worked closely together, and Max knew more than most about Evan's relationship with Angie.

"I wanted to ask you the same question. Something up with Noah?"

"In what way?"

"He's meeting with Angie?"

"You're jealous of Noah? The man's pushing sixty."

"Of course not. What's the matter with you?"

Max shrugged as he walked. "You're the guy asking questions."

"I got the impression something was off between them. A business something. Good grief, man. Jealous of Noah?"

This time Max grinned. "Well, we're all getting used to having her at the helm. It's funny. You moved into the big chair with barely a ripple whereas Angelica seems to be floundering."

"Floundering how? She understands every facet of the organization."

"I agree."

"She was all but running it before J.D. died She's smart. She's prepared. You all know she has J.D.'s blessing."

Max was quiet for a moment as they crossed an intersection. "Maybe it's the way she got here."

"You mean the way she tried to fight the will and teamed up with Jack Reed."

"I suppose. Or maybe we just geared up to follow you, and then bam, the world changed around us, and now we're all scrambling."

"She's going to do a great job," said Evan.

"I know she will. I have faith in her. But leadership's a tricky thing."

"How do you mean?"

They rounded a corner, making their way past one of the colorful eight-foot-tall cowboy-boot sculptures that dotted the city.

"When she seems to be going off in a risky direction, I'm not sure some of the older guys want to follow." Max held up his palms. "Don't get me wrong. I'm the integrated media guy. I'm all for going off in new directions."

"What do you mean, risky?" This was certainly news to Evan. Angie was stubborn, sure. But Lassiter Media was her life. He couldn't imagine she'd take risks with it.

"I'm talking about commissioning programming from non-Lassiter producers."

"You mean Conrad Norville?"

"According to Noah, it started with Conrad Norville, but now she's talking about making American versions of the top-rated affiliate programs."

Evan gave a laugh of comprehension. "She's eroding the powerbase of the existing Lassiter producers."

"And funding their competition. Like I said, I'm all for taking new directions. Heck, I think we should do a web-only series next summer. There's nobody internal who can produce that, so I'd be looking outside. But she's stepped into a minefield. Noah's not the only one who'll fight her."

"Who's on her side?"

"You mean, besides the British and Australian affiliates who'll get the licensing fees?"

"Yes. I mean, who's on her side in America."

"Me. And I assume, you? And, why haven't you guys talked about this?"

"I don't work at Lassiter anymore."

"But you're marrying the woman. Warn her. And why are you coming to me to—?" Max stopped in the middle of the sidewalk and turned to face Evan. "How is it that you don't know about this?"

Evan considered lying. Then he considered telling the truth. Neither was a realistic option. "It's complicated."

"Yeah. You said that. Complicated how?"

"You know what the family's been through."

Max thought for a moment. "But you're engaged again."

"She took back my ring."

"Have you set a date?"

"No."

Max watched Evan closely. "Is it better if I don't ask questions?"

"Yes."

Max gave a sharp nod. "I'm on her side, Evan. But I'm a director, and they're vice presidents."

"So, she's stepped into a hornet's nest?"

"Worse than that. She's busy breeding the hornets."

Seven

Angelica's day had been mentally exhausting. It was going to be harder than she'd expected to get the vice presidents on board. She could order them to commission non-Lassiter content, but that approach would be doomed to failure. It was hard enough to develop a successful television series, without having senior executives going reluctantly or half-heartedly into the effort.

It was dark when she parked her car in front of the house at Big Blue. She'd managed to put Evan out of her mind for most of the day. But now that she was home, memories of him were back, full blown in her mind.

She gripped the steering wheel for a long minute, willing away the sound of his voice, the tingle of his touch, the scent of his skin. They'd given into temptation last night, and she regretted it.

Though, in the light of day, she had realized the slipup was probably natural. Their relationship had ended so abruptly that there were bound to be lingering sexual urges. But that was all it had been. And it left her feeling hollow.

She eased the car door open and stepped out, looking toward the front porch. After a few seconds, she let her gaze wander to the pathway that led around back of the house.

There was nothing saying she had to go inside right away. She had no desire to face Evan, and she knew Marlene was bound to spot the engagement ring. It was pure, blind luck that she hadn't seen it last night.

Angelica truly wasn't ready for her aunt's excitement.

She firmly shut the car door then made her way along the pathway to the backyard. There, she made her way down the sloping lawn to the cottage that served as a pool house.

The large pool had been designed to blend in with the natural surroundings. Grass led up to its shallow edge, giving it the feel of a lake. She'd loved it here as a child, and she had happy memories of catapulting from the overhead tree swing. But tonight, all she wanted was to stretch out her muscles, burn off a little energy and postpone seeing anyone else for a little while longer.

It was a simple matter to find one of her bathing suits in the cottage. She changed, took a striped towel out to the deck, then waded into the cool, salt water. Goosebumps came up on her skin as she submerged. But once she started stroking her way across the deep end, she quickly warmed up.

She breathed deeply. Oxygen pumped its way through her limbs as she focused on putting power in her kicks and lengthening her strokes. She let her thoughts drift back in time and, eventually, both Evan and Lassiter Media vanished from her mind.

"We heard you drive up and wondered where you'd gone." Evan's voice interrupted her peace as she executed a turn.

Startled, she lost concentration and scraped her ankle.

"Marlene has dinner almost ready."

"I'll be up in a bit." Angelica determinedly pushed off the wall, leaving him behind.

He didn't take the hint and was still standing in the same spot silhouetted against the house when she returned.

"How did it go today?"

"Fine," she answered shortly. Then she turned to do another lap.

Again, he didn't go anywhere. "Something upsetting you?"

"No." She went under, holding her breath as long as possible, nearly making it back to the center of the pool before she came up for air.

At the end of her next lap, Evan was sitting on a deck chair.

"I'll meet you inside," she told him.

"I don't mind waiting."

"I might be a while."

He smiled in the dim light.

"What do you want, Evan?"

"To know how things went at Lassiter Media today." He glanced at his watch. "It's nearly seven."

"Your point?"

"It's late."

"There were a lot of people for me to see in Cheyenne."

"Socially?" he asked.

"Professionally."

"You do remember your father's will."

Angelica clamped her jaw, turning abruptly to start another lap. How dare Evan criticize her for working late. She'd worked until six tonight, merely an hour past regular quitting time. Big deal. Work-life balance was allowed to include work as well as life.

He was there when she returned.

"Swimming is life, not work," she told him.

"Did you have lunch?"

"What?"

"You heard me. Did you have lunch, or did you have meetings straight through?"

"We sent out." Somebody had brought in a platter of sandwiches during a noon-ish meeting.

"Did you eat?"

"Of course I ate."

She clearly remembered putting a turkey sandwich on her plate. She'd definitely had a drink of iced tea. But she'd been talking quite a lot at that point, and she couldn't say for certain how many bites she'd taken of the sandwich.

She did ten more laps without looking at him, but he still didn't leave.

Finally, she was forced to admit she was tired. Her arms and legs were beginning to feel like jelly. She waded out to the lawn, retrieving the fluffy towel she'd left on a lounger.

Evan approached. "You need anything out of the cabin?"

"I'll get it."

"Sure. Whatever."

She tucked the towel around herself sarong style and paced her way barefoot to the cabin. Evan walked alongside.

"How did it go today?" he asked again.

"I told you it was fine."

"You and Noah seeing eye to eye?"

"*You* and Noah ever see eye to eye?" she asked.

Everyone at Lassiter Media knew that Noah took a contrary position in most discussions. He seemed to like arguing.

"Occasionally," said Evan.

"I really don't want to talk about it." She entered the small cabin and retrieved her purse and clothes.

They walked along the concrete path to the house, but he continued to glance at her every few steps.

She stopped and turned to look at him. "Evan."

His gaze zeroed in on hers, and she lost her train of thought. Lassiter Media, Evan, their fights, making love, everything morphed together in a kaleidoscope in her head.

"Yes?" he prompted.

The silence stretched.

"I don't know," she finally admitted. "This is weird. It's all so incredibly confusing."

"I know. I really do. Tell me how it went today."

His tone was kind and there was concern in his eyes. And he was probably the one person in the world who did understand everything.

She gave in. "Not well. Not well at all. I hate to pull the gender card and say 'I can't get no respect because I'm a woman.' But I can't help but think he wouldn't react this way if I was J.D."

"Noah?"

"Yes," she admitted. "Noah."

"You're probably right about Noah's attitude," Evan agreed. "And maybe some of the other VPs, too. J.D. had the advantage of being experienced, venerated and male. But you have strengths he didn't, and you should learn to use them."

"What strengths?" she found herself asking. "What do I have that he didn't?"

"Vitality, fearlessness and youth."

"I suppose I'll eventually outlive Noah."

Evan grinned. "It is a good idea, though."

"What's a good idea?"

"Licensing hit series from the affiliates and remaking them in America."

Her suspicions instantly rose. "How did you know about that?"

"I asked around."

"You spied on me?"

"Of course I spied on you. If you don't want me to spy on you, then answer my questions when I ask."

"Evan, you can't spy on me."

"Actually, I'm pretty good at it."

"Angie?" Marlene's came down the patio stairs and took in Angelica's appearance. "Oh, good heavens, girl. Come inside. You're going to catch cold. I've got jambalaya and orange peel cookies."

Angelica felt her stomach rumble to life.

"I'm starving," Evan stated in a loud voice.

Marlene made her way down the stairs. "Let's get you into some dry clothes, young lady."

"Yes, ma'am," Angelica agreed. She had no intention of fighting with Evan in front of her aunt.

"Your fingers are turning bl—" Marlene gasped and lifted Angelica's left hand to gape at the ring. "Oh, my goodness." She looked to Evan, beaming with obvious happiness. "Oh, my goodness."

Angelica forced a smile, but her stomach went hollow around her lies. She couldn't imagine how she was ever going to extricate herself from all this.

Evan's heart went out to Angie, and he couldn't shake the feeling that he ought to apologize. Marlene had finally bid them good-night, but she'd left Angie looking positively shell-shocked amidst a cacophony of bride magazines, fabric swatches and invitation samples.

Through dinner, Marlene had ridden a crest of unbridled excitement at the idea of planning a new wedding. Though Angie protested that they hadn't even set a date, her aunt strongly recommended summer, outside, at Big Blue. And with that, she'd been off.

In the silence left in Marlene's wake, Angie zeroed in on Evan. "I can't believe you spied on me."

The accusation took him by surprise. "*That's* what you want to talk about?"

"I want to know where you get off interfering in Lassiter Media."

"What happened at Lassiter?" asked Tiffany. She and Deke were lounging at opposite ends of a big brown leather sofa.

"Forget Lassiter," said Deke. "It looks like The Wedding Show exploded all over Angelica."

She glared at him. "Not funny."

Tiffany covered a grin.

"Stop," said Angie.

"I'm sorry," said Tiffany. "I know it's not funny. But I can't help thinking there's a reality TV show in this somewhere."

"Reluctant brides?" asked Angie, looking like she might be considering it for a Lassiter channel.

But she quickly returned her accusatory glare to Evan.

He held up his hands in surrender. "Believe me, if I knew how to slow Marlene down, I'd do it."

"I'm not worried about Marlene." She paused. "Okay, I am worried about Marlene. But I'm more worried about Lassiter Media at the moment."

"I can help you with that," said Evan.

"I don't need your help."

"I'm the guy who set up the acquisitions in Britain and Australia. I know all the players."

"My problem isn't with Britain and Australia. It's with Noah, and the last thing I need is some man riding to my rescue. That'll only compound the problem." She came to her feet.

"So, what's your next move?" Evan asked.

"Are you kidding me?" She looked at Deke. "Is he kidding me? What part of *none of your business* don't you understand?"

Instead of answering, Deke took Tiffany's hand. "We should go to bed. These two need to talk."

Tiffany snapped her hand back. "Nice try."

"I didn't mean it that way." But his smirk said otherwise.

"Yeah, you did. But you're right. Angie, you guys need to talk. I wasn't in favor of this ruse, but now that it's gotten away from you, you better come up with an exit strategy."

"Maybe we can stay engaged for a while after Matt and Kayla's wedding," Evan offered.

"And draw this out?" Angie blinked at him in obvious dismay.

"That's our cue," said Deke, rising and drawing Tiffany to her feet.

"It would give people time to get used to our breakup," said Evan.

As Deke and Tiffany headed for the grand staircase, Evan moved to an armchair closer to Angie.

She was twisting the engagement ring around on her finger. "I can't believe we got ourselves in this deep."

"It seemed like a good idea at the time," he said. "And it worked. We got Conrad's mansion for Matt and Kayla."

"That's true. I am glad about that. But talk about unexpected consequences." She flopped back in the big chair.

"No good deed goes unpunished?"

"Something like that. And now I can't shake this nagging fear that we'll tell one or two more lies and accidentally end up married."

Evan chuckled at the joke, but something inside him warmed to the idea. Oh, he knew it was impossible, but as he gaze flicked to the wedding gowns pictured in the magazines left open on the coffee table, he acknowledged there was something compelling about Angie as a real bride, his bride.

"I've been thinking about the affiliates' top shows," Evan said, changing the topic. "*The Griffin Project* and *Cold Lane Park* would both be good choices for remakes."

"Traditional cop shows?" she asked, frowning.

"Tried and true. They're incredibly popular."

She seemed to forget to tell him to back off. "I was thinking something more cutting-edge, maybe super heroes or criminal procedural."

"*Alley Walker*?" he asked. "It's doing okay in Australia, but viewership has leveled off."

"We could use a younger hero, introduce a love interest. It's got that nice, edgy, paranormal aspect to it. And the leather outfit could reel in the teenage girls."

"If you had exactly the right actor," he mused.

"Eighteen to twenty-five demographic," said Angie. "That's where we need to focus."

Evan didn't disagree, but it was a tough audience to gauge. "What do you think of Max Truger?"

The question obviously took her by surprise. "In what way?"

"Is he doing a good job?"

"I guess." She sat forward and began stacking the bridal magazines.

"I was thinking he was young, and if that's where you want to focus, he might make a good VP."

Angie glanced up. "Are you telling me how to reorganize Lassiter Media?"

"I'm saying I buy into your vision of reaching a younger demographic."

She smacked the stack of magazines with energy and purpose. "And now you feel compelled to instruct me on how to do that?"

"Why are you so touchy? You're reacting emotionally to a perfectly logical suggestion."

"Because I'm a woman?"

Evan clamped his jaw and counted to five. "I'm not Noah."

"You sure sound like Noah."

"Well, I hope you don't sound like this when you're talking to him."

She rose up, her eyes darkening to burnt chocolate, and he immediately regretted the outburst. He didn't think she was a hysterical woman. He knew her to be cool, controlled and intelligent.

He stood with her. "I'm sorry. We've both had a long day. I know you're good at your job."

To his surprise, her features smoothed out, eyes cooling to their normal bronze. At first he was relieved. But then he realized it meant she'd withdrawn. He couldn't help but miss the emotion.

"You're right," she told him in a crisp tone. "This isn't a good time to discuss anything. Not that there'll ever be a good time for you and me to discuss anything about Lassiter Media. I've done all I can here in Cheyenne. We'll fly back to L.A. in the morning and get this wedding over with. After that, I can turn all of my attention to Lassiter."

He didn't like the single-minded determination in her eyes. "That's not what your father wanted, Angie."

"Are you *trying* to pick another fight?"

"I thought you were getting that now. He was truly worried about you. You should take another day, stay in Cheyenne and do something fun. Ride a horse or walk in the woods. Don't even go into the office."

She gave her hair a little toss. "I have too much work to do in L.A."

"That there is exactly why he was so worried. There will always be more work that needs doing. It's not a goal line, Angie. It's a treadmill. And you have to be really careful about letting the speed go up."

"There was and *is* absolutely nothing for my father or anyone else to worry about. I love my job, and I have it all under control."

She started to move, but he reached out to her, his hand landing on her elbow.

"This isn't about you controlling Lassiter Media. It's about Lassiter Media controlling you."

"Let go of me, Evan."

He searched her remote expression. "I need you to think about that."

"You lost the right to need anything from me a long time ago." She shook him off and turned on her heel.

As he watched her walk away, he couldn't help thinking he still needed a lot of things from her. Lovemaking was only the first on the list.

Thunder woke Angelica from a fitful sleep. Rain clattered on the roof above her, spraying in through the open window. She pulled back her covers and got up, crossing the room. As she wrestled the window closed, cold rain dampened her tank top and the soft pair of shorts she wore as pajamas.

Lightning flashed above the hills, illuminating both the sky and the ranch yard. She knew her cousin Chance and all the hands would be up and outside working, checking on the animals, securing anything that might blow away. The power could easily go out, but the ranch had emergency generators. When the weather turned nasty, the ranchers were in better shape than most people in town.

She shook rain droplets from her fingers, catching a glimpse of Evan's ring. She'd meant to take it off before bed, but somehow she'd forgotten. She touched it now as the lightning flashed off the diamond and thunder shook the big house.

She was angry with Evan for trying to interfere in Lassiter Media. Worse, his suggestions showed a complete lack of trust in her judgment. Didn't he remember that she'd all but run the company while her father was still alive?

During her conversation with Noah today, she'd realized the senior executives didn't have faith in her abilities. They were fine when they assumed J.D. was behind the scenes, vetting her decisions and actions. But now that she was on her own, they were questioning her.

A soft knock sounded on her door.

"Angie?" It was Tiffany's voice.

"Come on in," Angelica called.

The door cracked open. "Did the storm wake you too?"

"It did."

Tiffany moved through the doorway, her worried expression highlighted as another streak of lightning flashed through the sky.

"Are we in danger?" she asked.

"We're fine." Angelica flicked on a small lamp. "It's a powerful storm. But we get those every once in a while. Biggest problem is that it scares the cattle and blows everything all over the yard. But Chance and the hands will take care of that."

"That's a lot of rain." Tiffany sat down on the end of the bed, curling her bare feet beneath her. Like Angelica, she'd substituted casual clothes for pajamas, wearing a pair of black yoga pants and a cropped T-shirt.

"Something's sure to flood. Probably the ponds in the lower field. Hopefully, it won't be too hard on Marlene's vegetable garden." Angelica returned to the bed, popping her pillow against the white wooden headboard to lean back. "How'd it go with Evan after we left?"

"Predictable," said Angelica. "He thinks he's right, and I think he's wrong."

"Did you talk about your fake engagement?"

Angelica shook her head. "Mostly about Lassiter Media and what he thinks I should do there. He just can't help poking his nose into it. I don't need his advice. He needs to back off and let me work."

"I think he's trying to help."

"Whose side are you on?"

"Yours, absolutely. I'm just wondering why else he'd do it."

"It's a compulsion. Do you know how many times I wanted to call him up over the past six months and tell him he was crazy?" Angelica couldn't seem to stop herself from smiling at the memory. "I still had spies, you know. My dad might have taken me out of the CEO chair, but many people were loyal. They told me what Evan was doing with the British network purchase, then the Australian one. He spent a whole lot of corporate money in a very short time."

Lighting flashed and thunder boomed all around the house as the storm increased in intensity. Footsteps sounded on the stairs and on the floor below, and muffled voices sounded in the foyer. It would be all hands on deck outside.

It was coming up on 3:00 a.m. In another hour or so, Marlene would get up and start cooking in the kitchen; she'd be ready with food for anyone who needed sustenance. Angelica would go down to help. In addition to their efforts in the main house, the cook shack would already be humming with activity. Cowboys needed plenty of coffee, eggs, sausage and biscuits to keep them going in this.

"Was he wrong?" Tiffany asked.

"Hmmm?"

"Was Evan wrong to buy the networks?"

"I thought so then. And I'm still worried. But right or wrong, it is what it is. We now own those affiliates, and we need to do the best we can within that reality."

"Do you think he had a long-term vision?"

"What I think is that he's an empire builder. Even Lassiter Media wasn't big enough for him. He had to try to increase the size."

"I think he likes you."

The unexpected comment threw Angelica. "What?"

"I was watching him watch you tonight. I think he's still attracted to you."

"Physically maybe." Physically, Angelica still had it bad for Evan.

"Did he kiss you again?"

Angelica debated how much to tell Tiffany.

"Angie?"

"He kissed me again." She tippy-toed up to the truth.

"When? Where?"

"On the patio. Last night."

"Did you like it?"

Angelica hung her head and gave a sigh of defeat. "I always like it."

"How many times has it happened now?"

"Twice. Well, three times. Four if you count the one at the fitting."

Tiffany leaned in. "Big kisses? Small kisses? Give me some context here."

Angelica looked up. She realized she didn't want to lie or hold back. "Big kisses. Lots of them. So many that I lost count."

Tiffany's brows shot up.

"Especially last night. A dozen, a hundred, I don't know."

Tiffany's voice rose. "A *hundred?*"

"Shhh."

"I don't think they can hear me over the thunder. *A hundred?*"

"We had sex." It felt good to blurt it out.

Tiffany blinked. "You don't mean last night."

"I do."

Tiffany opened her mouth, then she closed it again. Thunder rumbled ominously.

"I know. I know." Angelica waved away the inevitable criticism. "It was a colossally stupid thing to do."

"I'm stunned."

"So was I."

"You…like…I mean…how…?"

"I'm weak," Angelica confessed. "He's a good-looking, sexy guy. And it's been a very long time since anyone held me close. And it was so easy, so familiar, so…unbelievably good." She fisted her hands around her quilt and squeezed in frustration.

"Uh oh."

"You have a gift for understatement."

"So, now what?"

"Now, nothing. We agreed to forget it ever happened."

"And how's that working for you?"

"Not well," Angelica admitted. "I didn't fall in love with him because he was a jerk. He's a good guy. We might not have been able to survive everything that came at us. But they were extraordinary circumstances. And, truth is, I don't know that he did all that much wrong."

Tiffany stretched out on her stomach on the far side of the bed, propping her elbows on the mattress and her chin on her hands. "You ever think about trying this reconciliation for real?"

"No. *No.* Not at all. Too much has happened, Tiff. When push came to shove, I—" Angelica swallowed, suddenly afraid she might cry. "I let him down." She drew a shaky breath. "He won't forgive me. He can't forgive me."

"Maybe you should—"

"No!" Angelica gave an adamant shake of her head. "I missed my chance with Evan. I've got Lassiter Media to think about now. It's going to take all of my focus. I'm not going to delude myself into dreaming about anything else."

"I suppose." Tiffany's agreement seemed reluctant.

There was a banging on the door.

"Angelica?" This time, it was Deke.

"Come in," she called.

Deke swung the door wide. "I just talked to Evan. He said to tell you they're sandbagging Williams Creek."

Angelica rolled off the bed and came to her feet. "Are they worried about the road?"

Deke nodded.

"It hasn't flooded there in years." While she talked, she pulled open a drawer and threw a sweatshirt on.

"It's risen two feet at Norman Crossing."

"What do we do?" asked Tiffany from behind her.

Angelica tossed her a warm shirt. "We can go help sand-bag. Last time this happened, the only way we could get to town for over a week was by off-road, four-wheel drive."

Evan couldn't help but be impressed by the way the Cheyenne ranchers pulled together in a time of crisis. There were at least fifty people out in the pouring rain, and they'd been working at it for hours. Men, women and teenagers lined the creek bank, filling bags from the back of a pickup then moving them in human chains to the low section of the road where it paralleled the creek.

Evan was working with Deke and Chance at the leading edge of the barrier, stacking the largest sandbags in a base layer, while Angie worked in a small group farther upstream, finishing off the top layer. Even from here, she looked exhausted. Her raincoat was plastered to her body. The hood had long since fallen down, and her hair was dark and stringy, making her face look pale.

He longed to go to her, pull her into her arms and escort her someplace warm and dry. But he knew she wouldn't stop working. Many of the women had already taken breaks, including Tiffany, who'd all but fallen over before one of the ranchers had dragged her off to sit on the hillside and drink a cup of coffee. But Angie hadn't slowed down. She'd been plugging away, sandbag after sandbag.

Refocusing, he went back to work, building the foundational layer, making sure it was solid.

When he looked up again, Angie was farther upstream. She seemed to be on her own, doing a final check of the barrier's integrity. The others were making their way back.

Evan was reminded that the woman he'd first met at a social event, then came to know in the boardroom and escorted to L.A.'s hotspots, had also spent a good deal of her life on a working ranch. She was used to physical work, and would step in and help out wherever she was needed. He stopped feeling sorry for her, and started being impressed.

Chance suddenly grasped Evan's arm, squeezing it tight. "Do you hear that?" he called out, drawing Deke's attention as well.

Evan listened. His heart sank. A low, ominous rumble was coming from upstream.

"Get back! Quick!" Chance shouted to everyone, urging people to run. "Across the road! Up the bank! Everybody *move*, now!"

Deke echoed the call, as did Evan, rushing along the creek, ordering everyone back from the bank. The sound was growing louder, and Evan could see a roiling flood of water and debris barreling down on them.

"Angie!" he cried out.

She was the farthest away, cut off from safety by the curve of the creek and a grove of trees. She was running toward him, and he broke into a faster sprint along the rocky bank.

"Go," she cried out to him, motioning for him to get to safety. "I'm coming."

But she wasn't fast enough. He could see the water rushing up behind her.

"Run," he cried out to her, pumping up his own speed.

Then she tripped. She went down on the rocks, and his heart stopped in his chest. While she lay motionless, everything inside him screamed in agony.

"Angie!"

Eight

Evan had thirty feet to go to get to her, then twenty, then ten.

She sat up and rose unsteadily to her feet.

He finally reached her, wrapped an arm firmly around her waist, all but carrying her as they headed for the road and the safety of the bank beyond. Fifty sets of eyes were riveted to their progress.

"My shoulder," she gasped.

"Hang on." There wasn't a second to lose.

Chance started toward them, but then he looked past Evan, and his face turned ashen. Evan knew exactly what the other man was seeing—soupy, gray water laced with rocks, tree trunks and branches about to overtake them. It wasn't humanly possible to outrun it.

Quickly changing tactics, he hauled Angie to the nearest tree. He grabbed her thighs and hoisted her up as high as he could reach.

"Grab on," he called. "Grab anything."

"I got it," she shouted back, using one hand to pull her butt onto a wide branch and scrambling for a foothold.

He was out of time.

The freezing, debris-ridden water engulfed him. He instinctively took a deep breath, closed his eyes and wrapped his arms around the tree trunk, holding on for dear life.

The trunk protected his face and body from direct hits, but branches battered him on all sides, scratching his arms, bruising his legs, bouncing off his shoulders and hips.

His lungs were about to burst, when the water receded. He sucked in air.

"Evan!" Angie's cry seemed high above him.

But then the water closed in again.

This time, he couldn't fight the cold. It was numbing his fingers, making it impossible to hang on. Deep down in the base of his brain, he realized he was running out of time. Angie was safe, he told himself. At least Angie was safe.

The water receded again, and he drew another breath.

"Climb," Angie called to him. "Climb, Evan!"

The water was at his neck. He opened his eyes, and his brain registered the chaos around him, foaming water clogged with debris. The sandbag wall had disappeared, as had part of the road. But the sandbagging crew was high on the bank, out of harm's way.

"Come on, Evan," Angie shouted. "Get up here."

He gritted his teeth and reached one arm up. He managed to grasp a branch. It bit into his freezing hand, and it was all he could do to hang on. But he reached up with his other hand, getting it slightly higher. His feet scrambled along the trunk. Then one of them connected with a foothold. He pushed with all his might, grabbing a higher branch, then another and another.

His body finally cleared the water, and he heaved himself onto a broad branch next to Angie.

"Thank God," she breathed. Her face was wet and pale, her right hand clinging to the tree, her left arm dangling by her side.

"Damn," he ground out.

"You okay?" she asked.

"Forget me." He eased his way toward her. "Your shoulder's dislocated."

"You nearly died."

"I'm fine. Dammit." He knew she had to be in agonizing pain.

She swallowed. Then her teeth started to chatter, and her eyes went glassy.

"I think I can help you." He reached forward.

"Don't touch me," she begged.

"You have to trust me."

"They'll come and get me. Chance will have called the medics by now."

He continued inching himself toward her. People on the bank were calling out to them, and the water continued to roar beneath them. They rain pounded down, but Evan's focus was completely on Angie.

"I'm going to wrap my arm around your waist."

"Evan, don't."

He did it anyway. "Relax, Angie. If your muscles are relaxed, you're going to feel better."

"I can wait."

"I know it hurts like hell."

"I'm fine."

He put his other hand gently on the forearm of her injured side. "Relax," he whispered in her ear. "Please sweetheart, just relax and trust me."

"Okay," she whispered. Then she gave a shaky nod.

"I'm going to move your arm slowly and gently. I won't do anything sudden." He kept talking as he worked, hoping to distract her. "You're right. They are coming for us. Help is going to be here soon, and you'll be home and dry in no time." He bent her elbow, pivoting her forearm. "I bet Marlene will make hot chocolate, with whipped cream, and cookies. She'll have been baking all day." He eased her shoulder out straight. "I hope she made monster cookies. Oatmeal and pecans, they really stick to your ribs." He moved her arm higher pivoting the shoulder.

She gasped a breath, but then the shoulder popped back into place.

She gave a small exclamation of pain.

"That's it," he quickly told her. "It's back in."

Angie relaxed against him, gasping in deep breaths.

"How does it feel?"

"Quite a lot better."

He gave in to impulse and kissed the top of her head. "Good."

"You just saved my life."

"You climbed the tree with a dislocated shoulder. I just gave you a shove."

She was quiet for a moment.

"Evan?" Chance called, his voice loud and worried. He was as close to them as he could get without wading into the overflowing creek. "You guys okay?"

"We're good," Evan called back. "But Angie's going to need a doctor."

"What's wrong?"

"She hurt her shoulder. Nobody's bleeding. We're just cold."

"You're bleeding," said Angie.

Evan glanced down at his body. His sleeves and pants were torn, and several deep scratches oozed blood.

"It's not bad," he told her.

"I thought you were dead."

He gave a choppy laugh. "For a second there, it didn't look so good. But I'm fine. Clearly, I'm tough."

"You're tough," she agreed.

He glanced at the landscape around them. "This is a mess."

"I've never seen it this bad. I guess I won't be going back to L.A. today. You need a doctor."

"Not anymore. So, how did you learn to fix a dislocated shoulder."

He hesitated to tell her. "YouTube video."

"Is that a joke?"

"It's not."

"Weren't you worried you'd do it wrong?"

"A little," he admitted. "But I dislocated my shoulder when I was a teenager. So I know how it feels. I was more worried about you being in such terrible pain."

She seemed to think about it for a moment. "Well, I guess that's nice."

"How's it doing?"

She flexed it a little. "Much better. Maybe you should watch a brain surgery video next, since you learn things so quickly."

He liked that she was joking. "That way, if my business management gig doesn't work out, I'll have a fallback?"

"What's your business management gig?"

Evan shifted to a more comfortable position in their perch. "Can I trust you to keep it confidential?"

"Yes, you can."

"You won't go running to the tabloids like Conrad did?"

"I never talk to the tabloids. Though, maybe we should tell them about this." She cupped a hand around her mouth. "Hey, Chance!"

"What do you need?" her cousin called back.

"Get a picture of us, will you?"

Even from this distance, Evan could see Chance's grin. "We've already got about a hundred."

"A picture of all this should keep Conrad satisfied," Angie said to Evan. "Try to look ecstatic about saving my life."

"I am ecstatic about saving your life."

"That's the spirit."

"I *am*."

"Tell me about your business management gig."

"Okay. But it really is confidential."

"I understand."

"Lex, Deke and I are looking into buying the Sagittarius." The surprise was clear in her tone. "The resort?"

"That's the one."

"You're going to *run a hotel?*"

"We are."

"But…I mean, Lex I can see, but Deke? And *you?*"

"Your confidence is overwhelming."

"You know what I mean. You don't have any experience running hotels."

He frowned at her. "Seriously, Angie? 'You don't know what you're doing' is the thing you want to say to the guy who just saved your life?"

"You know what I mean. You didn't jump up and buy Lassiter Media. You spent years learning the ropes before you were in charge."

Evan supposed that was true enough. "And now I'll learn about hotels. Maybe there's a YouTube video available."

"So, you're using J.D.'s money?"

"I am. I haven't decided exactly how. I'm thinking about setting up a trust, using the money as a shareholder loan, and then donating the proceeds to a worthy cause."

"Why not just put it in as equity?"

"Because it feels like a bribe, like your father paid me to mess with your head. I hate that, Angie. I never, *ever* would have agreed to a scheme like that."

Sirens sounded in the distance, and flashing lights appeared down the road.

"Looks like the cavalry is here," said Angie.

"I hope they brought a boat."

Angelica felt like she'd been transported back in time to her teenage years. It was nearly ten o'clock now, dark and raining outside, and further cleanup efforts were going to have to wait until morning. In the great room at Big Blue, Marlene was handing around steaming mugs of hot chocolate. Chance was regaling them with stories of action, hard work and heroism, not the least of which was Evan's rescue of Angelica.

Happily nobody else had been injured in the flood, but several of the area ranches had been damaged. People were coming together to move livestock, drain fields, fix buildings, and make donations to their neighbors. The main road had been wiped out in a couple of places. Construction crews would arrive in the morning so that work could begin as soon as the rain stopped.

After taking an X-ray that confirmed Angelica's shoulder was correctly in place, the doctor had given her some pain pills and told her to take it easy for a week or so. She felt pleasantly tired and fuzzy as she moved her gaze past Chance to Evan. He had literally saved her life today, risking his own to do it. How did she thank him for that?

"How's the cocoa?" asked Tiffany, curling into a spot next to Angelica on the leather sofa.

A fire crackled in the big, stone fireplace and the aroma of fresh-made monster cookies wafted in from the kitchen. Rain splatted against the windows,

"Marvelous," Angelica answered, taking a sip.

"Was it like this while you were growing up?" Tiffany asked, glancing around at the homey atmosphere.

"Just like this," said Angelica. "I really miss it sometimes."

Tiffany cradled her own mug of cocoa. "We're definitely not in L.A."

"I like them both," said Angelica.

Though, at the moment, she preferred Cheyenne. She'd love to hole up here for a few more days and think about nothing at all.

"How are things between you and Evan?"

"Okay. Fine. He saved my life, so I guess I might have to forgive him for spying on me."

"You might," Tiffany agreed.

Angelica's memory went back to the moment he'd shoved her into the tree. "Do you think—?"

"What?"

"Well, I mean, do you think he'd have done that for anybody? He really could have died. He almost did."

While he held her dripping wet in his arms, Angelica had admitted to herself how much she missed him. Soon, once the wedding was over, he'd go off into the world and be somebody else's hero. The thought made her intensely sad.

"You know him better than I do," Tiffany answered softly.

"He would. He'd have risked his life to save anybody. He's that kind of a guy."

Tiffany put a hand on Angelica's good shoulder. Her voice was gentle. "Is this getting complicated?"

"It is."

"Are you going to get hurt?"

"Probably."

"Okay, but one small point to make here. You're a little high on painkillers right now. This might not seem as complex in the morning."

Angelica couldn't help but smile. "I hadn't thought of that."

"Plus, the man saved your life. You're probably experiencing some gratitude hormones."

"Is there such a thing?"

"I bet firefighters and police officers get laid all the time. Or, at least get offers. Though I imagine they're professionally obligated to say no."

Angelica could well believe they got offers. In the aftermath of the flood, she'd have hopped into bed with Evan in a heartbeat.

His gaze suddenly caught and held hers from across the

room, well out of hearing distance. His smile was slow and tender, and a wave of emotion clogged her chest. Again, she went back in time, to when they were engaged, happy and in love. Those moments had been incredibly precious, yet she'd taken them for granted.

Evan said something to Chance, then crossed the over to her.

"Want me to leave?" asked Tiffany.

Angelica grasped her hand. "Stay."

"You got it. Hi, Evan."

"How are you doing, Tiffany?"

"Tired," she replied. "I haven't worked that hard in years. Well, maybe never."

Evan gave her an answering smile. "I don't imagine sandbagging comes up very often in corporate real estate."

"I once had to call a plumber to fix a kitchen faucet, but that's as close as I've come to flood control."

Evan turned his attention to Angelica. "How about you?"

"I'm high on pain killers."

"So now would be a good time to ask you a favor?"

A flutter of nerves passed through her stomach. "That depends."

"Don't look so scared. It's nothing too painful."

"But I won't like it."

"Probably not. Let me help you with Noah."

She didn't even consider it. "No."

"You're going to see him again before you leave Cheyenne?"

"I plan to."

Evan perched on an armchair at the corner of the sofa. "I genuinely want you to succeed, Angie."

"I am going to succeed." In case nobody had noticed, she was the CEO. She could, in fact, make unilateral decisions if she wanted.

"I can help."

Tiffany stepped in. "I don't think Angie should be arguing right now. She should be resting."

"You're right," said Angelica, taking the opportunity to exit the conversation. "I should go to bed."

She didn't want to fight with Evan. But she didn't want to give in to him either. Though she hated to admit it, at the moment, a little help with Noah seemed like a good idea. And that was clearly a dangerous line of thinking.

She polished off her hot chocolate and rose to her feet.

Saying goodnight to everyone, she made her way to her bedroom. Her shoulder was tender, but she managed to get out of her shirt and bra and into a clean tank top. It was a bit of a chore to wash up and comb her hair, but she managed.

Once she was ready for bed, she sat down to reassemble her cell phone. She'd opened it up and pulled out the battery and SIM card in an attempt to dry everything out. She pressed the On button and was happy to see the screen light up. Satisfied, she set the alarm and crawled into bed.

Her quilt was warm, her pillow soft, and a lighter rain now drummed above her. The pain pills had done their job, and her shoulder was no longer throbbing. She floated quickly into sleep.

What seemed like only moments later, her phone rang.

Angelica dragged her eyes open, squinting at the screen to find it was barely after eleven at night. The number was Kayla's, so she picked it up.

"Hello?"

"Angie? It's Kayla. You okay?"

"A little groggy. But good, yeah." Angelica let her head drop back on the pillow.

"We saw the flood footage on LNN. Is Big Blue okay? Any damage?"

"Very little here. We're just soggy. It rained and rained. In fact, it's still raining."

"We've booked a flight to Cheyenne in the morning.

We're coming home to help. The Dysons got hit pretty bad, and I heard the hospital is going to need a new generator."

"The community is pulling together."

"I know. And we want to be there."

Angelica understood the sentiment. She was going to have to return to L.A. soon, but she'd stay as long as she could, and Lassiter Media would make a hefty donation to the reconstruction effort.

"I'm sorry to call so late," Kayla continued. "But I wanted to let you know right away, and to tell you personally." She seemed to hesitate. "With all this going on. Well, Matt and I were talking, and…it doesn't seem like the right time to have a splashy, Malibu Beach wedding."

Angelica sat up, wincing as the movement stretched her shoulder. *"What?"*

"We're thinking of postponing. We need to be in Cheyenne, and we can't be there and still be planning the wedding here. I know how hard you've worked." Kayla's tone was apologetic.

Angelica scrambled to recover. "It's not about me. It's your wedding. You should do what feels right."

Kayla let out a relieved sigh. "I just couldn't do it. I couldn't sip champagne in a three-thousand-dollar dress while our friends and neighbors back home were struggling to restore power and water."

"I understand," said Angelica. She truly did.

"Matt is calling Conrad Norville, and the caterers, and the florist, and the musicians. But can you let Evan know?"

Angelica swallowed. "Sure."

"Thanks. And thank you so much for understanding. Will you still be in Cheyenne tomorrow?"

"I will," said Angelica. "For a couple more days, anyway."

"That's great. I'll call you when we get there."

"Good. Great. I'll talk to you tomorrow."

"Bye," said Kayla.

Angelica set down her phone and swung her legs from under the covers. She was guessing Kayla expected her to simply roll over and tell Evan about the cancellation. Since she thought they were back together again, it made sense Kayla would expect them to be sleeping together.

She sighed and rose to her feet. The house was silent. Not surprising, since everyone would have an early morning and a busy day tomorrow. She didn't know Deke's plans, but she'd overheard Evan last night offering to help.

No wedding, she said to herself as she padded to her bedroom door. *No wedding*, she repeated, opening the door and slipping through, heading down the great staircase. Okay, so no wedding.

She made her way through the kitchen, back to the guest room where Evan was staying. She knew her way blindfolded, but light from the yard filtered through the big windows, making it easy to see her way. Pale light was visible under Evan's door, meaning he was likely still awake.

She knocked lightly.

"Yes?" he called from within.

She cracked open the door. "It's me."

A small bedside lamp was on. "Angie? What's wrong? Are you in pain?"

"I'm fine," she assured him, opening the door wider and going inside.

"You sure?" He closed a book and set it on the night table.

She shut the door behind her and nodded as she crossed the room. The floor was cold under her bare feet, so she perched on the end of his bed, pulling her soles from the floor.

"What's going on?" he asked.

"Kayla called."

He waited.

"They saw footage of the flood. They're coming back to Cheyenne."

"I'm not surprised."

"And they're canceling the wedding."

Evan drew back against the headboard. "Canceling it how?"

"They don't want a posh party in Malibu while there are people in trouble in Cheyenne."

"I guess I can understand that."

Their gazes met and locked. Then his dropped to her left hand, and the engagement ring.

"So," he ventured, "I guess our secret plan—"

"Was a very big waste—"

"Of time."

"I was going to say effort."

"That too." He raked a hand over his short hair.

"Not to mention all the lies." She reached for the ring, pulling it from her finger.

But he sat forward, his hand closing over hers, stopping the action. "Don't."

She looked up in confusion.

"Breaking it off now is going to seem very abrupt."

"So what? It's not like there's going to be a better time."

"People have enough to worry about already."

"The two of us pretending to stay together is not going to help the flood reconstruction."

"That's true," he agreed. But he didn't remove his hand. "What about Lassiter Media?"

She felt her guard go up. "What about it?"

"You've already got trouble with Noah. You're trying to build credibility and trust. How's it going to look if you get reengaged for a few days and then change your mind?"

"Who says it's me changing my mind? Maybe it was you who broke it off."

"That'll make them ask why."

"Evan, for goodness' sake."

"If I break it off, you run the risk of people thinking I had a reason."

"How is that fair?"

"Gossip's never fair. And you're more of a celebrity than me. Who do you think will be the target?"

She had to admit, he had a point. Not that she was agreeing with the idea. She rubbed her hands up and down her chilled arms. "We can't just stay engaged."

He shrugged. "We can for a while."

"How long is a while? Or maybe we should just get married." Her voice went higher as she spoke. "That would really throw them off. If we actually went through with the wedding, who would ever suspect the engagement was a sham?"

"There's no need to be sarcastic."

"Yes, there is. We have an honest-to-God problem here."

"And we have an honest-to-God, if temporary, solution. I'm not saying forever, Angie. We can shut it down anytime we want. But not tonight. Not tomorrow. Let's let a few of these other things work themselves out first. It'll be easier that way."

"You think this is easy?"

It sure wasn't easy for her, spending time with Evan, talking to him, laughing with him, experiencing his little touches in front of Marlene and others to keep up the charade. Every minute of every day, she remembered more and more about their life together. She remembered why she'd fallen in love with him, and how badly it had hurt to lose him.

She shivered at the memory.

"Cold?" he asked.

She didn't answer, but she was. Her shorts and tank top didn't give much warmth.

He pulled back the covers. "Hop in."

"Are you *crazy?*"

"You're injured. You're doped up. And you're freezing. I think I can manage to be a gentleman for a few minutes."

She hesitated, but the promise of warmth was too much to ignore. She scooted up to sit next to him, and he flipped the covers over her legs. They weren't touching, but the warmth of his skin swirled out to her.

"Better?" he asked.

She nodded.

"We don't say anything for a few days."

"I don't like it."

"I know you don't. I don't blame you."

"What about you?" she asked. "This can't be any fun for you either."

He angled his body to look at her. "I really don't mind. It's not like I have a girlfriend to worry about. And I like your family."

"But you have to hang around with me. You have to pretend…"

"That I like you? I've always liked you, Angie. You might be kind of quirky and misguided."

"*Excuse* me?"

"And you nearly got me killed today."

"Okay, that part's true."

"But, all in all, you're not that objectionable."

She whacked him in the thigh, realizing too late she'd used her sore arm. She groaned in pain.

He was instantly concerned. "You okay?"

"No. I'm an idiot. Ouch."

"It's the drugs. You're a bit addled right now."

"Is that why I'm agreeing to stay engaged to you?"

"No, that's the smart part of your brain talking."

The throbbing was subsiding in her shoulder. "What's in it for you?"

"I'm still hoping to help with Noah."

"I'm not going to let you. Besides, that would technically be for me. And why do you want to do it anyway?"

He gently wrapped an arm around her shoulders. "I was

in love with you once, Angie. Very, very much in love with you. And feelings like that don't just evaporate into thin air."

She knew what he meant. She felt it too. She tried to frame it in words. "Ghost feelings."

"That's right. You're haunting me."

"You're haunting me too," she admitted.

He squeezed her ever so gently. "Maybe that's why we made love."

A flush warmed her body. It was the first time either of them had mentioned it.

"I guess," she said.

His tone went low. "For a few minutes there, it was as if we'd never been apart."

She was afraid to answer, because she agreed.

The air thickened between them.

He reached over to smooth back her hair. Then he brushed the pad of his index finger along her cheek. He looked deeply and intensely into her eyes. "No one would ever know."

Arousal throbbed in the depths of her body, heating to life. She understood what he meant. If they did it again, no one would ever know. And what could it change? They'd already given in once. It hadn't made things better, but then it hadn't made things a whole lot worse either. She was as confused and conflicted before making love to him as she had been after.

He kissed her oh so tenderly on the lips. "Tell me if I hurt you. Tell me if I hurt you, and I'll stop."

Nine

With an arm around her waist, Evan eased Angie down into his bed. Her tank top shimmied up, exposing her flat stomach, her smooth skin. She was everything he'd ever remembered and loved.

"You're so beautiful," he breathed.

"And you're so strong." Her palms skimmed his bare shoulders, moving along his biceps.

He was wearing boxers, but nothing else.

She frowned as she took in his torso. "You really got hurt out there."

"Just scrapes and bruises. They'll heal."

"They look painful. I'm afraid to touch you."

"Please don't be afraid of that." He settled his palm against her bare stomach. "Because I'm dying to touch you."

He brought his lips to hers again, hoping to reassure her. The last thing he wanted was for her to have second thoughts. It had been months since she'd been in his bed. And now that she was here, he realized how desperately he wanted her this way.

She accepted his kiss. Then she kissed him back. Her arms wound around him, her small, soft hands coming up against his back.

Conscious of her shoulder, he hugged her around the waist, bringing them together, her softness against his tension. He deepened the kiss, and her tongue answered his, sending sweeps of passion through his body, pushing every other thought from his mind.

Angie. This was Angie in his bed again, finally.

He let his hand slide up and skim the side of her breast, which was bare beneath the tiny tank top. Then he moved on to her shorts, running his fingers over her hip, the curve of her rear, the smoothness of her bare thigh. She curled her body against him. The sensation was so familiar his throat went raw.

"I've missed you," he moaned.

Her hand framed his chin, and she kissed him deeply. "This is so confusing."

"It's going to be okay. I promise."

On some level, he realized his words made no sense. But he wanted it to be true. He desperately hoped he'd never have to hurt her again.

She slipped off her tank top, a little awkwardly around her sore shoulder. But she'd revealed her beautiful breasts, and that was all he cared about. He settled her skin against his, absorbing her warmth and softness.

She kissed her way along his bruised chest. "Am I hurting you?"

"You're healing me."

There was a smile in her voice as her lips brushed his skin. "I don't think sex has any medicinal properties."

"Let's test that theory."

Impatient to have her naked, he stripped off her little shorts and tossed them aside. Then he kicked out of his boxers. In seconds, they were full length, skin to skin. He rolled slowly onto his back, bringing her with him.

"Tell me if anything hurts," he said.

"Nothing hurts." She gave him a lingering kiss. "I can't feel a thing."

"That's disappointing." He slipped his hand between her thighs. "Can you feel that?"

She gave a low moan.

He caressed her more intimately. "That?"

"Oh, Evan."

His breathing grew ragged as his arousal ramped up. "That?" he managed.

She hugged him more tightly, and buried her face in the crook of his neck. "Don't stop. Don't— Oh, my."

Unable to wait a second longer, he guided himself inside. The moist warmth of her body closed around him, sending lasers of arousal sweeping through his brain.

He tried desperately to take it slow, but it wasn't going to work.

It was impossible to talk. He guided her onto her back.

"It's good," she assured him as she sank back into the mattress. "So good."

She arched her hips against him, and he braced himself on his forearms. He gazed at her beautiful, flushed face, as his body went on autopilot. Her eyes were closed, lashes thick against her creamy skin. Her hair was mussed and sexy. Her cheeks were pink, lips full, red and slightly parted. He could get aroused simply by looking at her.

A moan escaped from her lips, and her legs wrapped around him. She arched her hips further, ankles locking in the small of his back. He'd wanted to be gentle, promised himself he'd be careful, but his instincts had been hijacked by need, and his body pumped faster and faster.

"Evan!" she finally cried out, head tipping back into the pillow.

He felt her shudder and convulse. He was instantly over the edge, ecstasy pairing with oblivion in huge waves that rocked his body to the core.

It took a long time to recover, before he could move, before he had the presence of mind to turn them over so that he didn't give in and crush her to the bed.

He lay back and dragged a quilt overtop of them. Her long hair tickled his neck as she rested her head on his chest. Her soft curves settled perfectly around the planes and angles of his body. Nothing hurt anymore, not in the slightest; he felt as though he was drifting on a plane of heaven.

He stroked her messy hair. "You're amazing." He wanted to say more. He wanted to marvel at how good they were together. Making love with Angie was like nothing else in the world. But that conversation would take them somewhere they couldn't afford to go. For now, it was enough that she was here in his arms.

Her fingertips traced a pattern on his chest. "I can't believe it was all for nothing."

"What's that?" He wondered if she meant the sandbags.

"Me, you, Conrad, the tabloids, my brothers, *Marlene*."

"Oh, that. Yeah, well, who could have predicted the flood of the century?"

"If we hadn't made up the story, hadn't lied to a single person, everything would have turned out exactly the same."

He disagreed. "If we hadn't lied, I never would have followed you to Cheyenne, and you might have been swept away by the flood."

"So our lies saved my life?"

"I'm going with that one."

She seemed to ponder for a moment. "If we hadn't lied, I wouldn't have talked to Conrad, and I wouldn't have come up with the idea of remaking the affiliate's hit shows. Then Noah and I wouldn't have disagreed, and I never would have been in Cheyenne yesterday."

"But it's a good idea," Evan countered. "If you don't do it, Lassiter Media could start losing market share. If you'd never come up with it, the company might have spiraled downward, eventually going bankrupt and taking the entire Lassiter empire with it."

He felt laughter rumble through her chest. It was another sensation that was achingly familiar.

"We've just saved the Lassiter empire by lying to my family and the entire world?"

"We never lied to Deke and Tiffany. But yeah."

Sleep was creeping into her voice. "You really do need to get yourself a white charger, Evan McCain."

"Your horse Delling is a dapple gray. That's pretty close."

Her voice got softer. "Too bad you didn't marry me. He'd have been half yours."

As she relaxed into sleep, the words bounced around inside Evan's brain. *Too bad you didn't marry me.*

If he could go back in time, he honestly might have dragged her to the altar.

Angelica crept back up to her bedroom at 6:00 a.m. Evan had roused her from a sound sleep to give her the choice— staying with him a while longer or going back to her own room before the family got up. For a split second, she'd been tempted to stay. But she knew it was a ridiculous impulse. They weren't a couple any longer.

She silently twisted her bedroom door handle, pushing the door inward on smooth hinges. Then she startled, sucking in a breath when she saw Tiffany sitting on her bed.

"You've been downstairs?" Tiffany asked, a suspicious expression in her eyes.

"Kayla called." Angelica silently closed the door behind her, leaning back against it. "I had to talk to Evan. They've canceled the wedding."

Tiffany rolled to her feet. "And how long did that take?"

Angelica thought about lying, but this was Tiffany. "About six hours."

Tiffany's expression softened. "You want to talk?"

"I don't know." Angelica honestly didn't. She crossed the room to her dresser, sliding open a drawer, realizing the logical thing to do was get dressed and go on with the day.

"If you did want to talk," Tiffany continued, moving toward her, "what would you want to say?"

Angelica gripped the half-open drawer, giving up on holding her emotions at bay. "That Evan is the best lover in the entire universe."

There was a split second pause. "Okay. Well. That's… uh…hmmm."

Angelica turned. "I couldn't agree with you more."

"What are you going to do?"

Excellent question. "First, I'm getting dressed." Angelica retrieved a pair of blue jeans and a hunter-green shirt from her drawer.

She stared at the clothing that she only used on visits to Big Blue. It suddenly felt like her past, and she tossed it onto the bed, not sure if she should wear it.

"No," she decided. "First, I'm going to brush my teeth."

"Okay. But what about the big question?"

"There is no big question. He didn't ask, and I didn't ask. Nothing's changed, Tiff. We just couldn't quite keep our hands off each other a couple of times."

Tiffany was silent for a moment. "I meant with Kayla and Matt. But please do continue talking about your sex life."

Angelica rolled her eyes, then pivoted and headed into the bathroom.

"They're coming to Cheyenne to help out," she called back. "They don't want to host a splashy wedding party while people are recovering."

"That makes sense," said Tiffany. "When you think about it, what else would people like Kayla and Matt do?"

"I know." Angelica nodded as she squeezed toothpaste onto her brush.

"Wait a minute." Tiffany appeared in the doorway. "That means you and Evan don't need to fake it any longer."

"That's what I told him last night."

"Yet somehow, you ended up sleeping with him instead? You want to walk me through that logic, Angie?"

Angelica held her toothbrush under the faucet. "He doesn't want it to be too sudden. For my family, mostly, especially for Marlene. He thinks we should let them down more gently. Plus, he thinks making up and breaking up in such rapid succession will make me look like a flake to the Lassiter Media brass." She shut off the tap. "I'm not sure he's wrong. I think I've already got trouble on that front."

Tiffany had moved to lean in the bathroom doorway, talking while Angelica brushed. "You're the Lassiter Media brass, Angie. You can tell them to stuff it."

Angelica knew it wasn't that easy. "My father handpicked those men. They're the backbone of the company."

"You're the head of the company. They have to follow you now."

Angelica spat and rinsed her brush. "I'm confident we'll get there. But they have to respect me, not fear me. The faster I can make that happen, the easier my job gets. It's true that looking like I have an erratic love life isn't going to garner me any respect."

"So, what's the long-term play here? Are you going to have to marry Evan so you don't look like a flake in front of the vice presidents?"

Angelica couldn't help laughing. "That's exactly what I said to Evan."

"What did he say?"

"He told me I was being sarcastic. I was. It wasn't helpful, but I was kind of rattled at the time."

"And then?"

"And then he told me I wasn't too objectionable, and he

could tolerate hanging around with me for a while longer, for the good of the cause."

A smirk grew on Tiffany's face. "Smooth talker. I can see why you jumped into bed with him."

"No, that happened when he said he'd once been very much in love with me, and feelings like that didn't evaporate into thin air."

Tiffany sobered. "Oh. Well, yeah. I can definitely see that working."

Angelica wandered back into the bedroom, plunking herself down on the bed next to her jeans. "I should know what to do here. I shouldn't feel so confused."

Tiffany sat down with her. "Do you want him back? Do you want to try again?"

"Setting aside for the moment that I not only burned that bridge, I blew it sky-high and buried the ashes, I'm not as sure as I once was that I don't want him back."

Tiffany blinked for a moment. "Let's pretend I actually followed that train of logic. You're saying you might want him back?"

"I'm saying I no longer know that I don't."

"You've been talking to too many reporters."

"I don't know. I'm confused." Angelica snagged a pillow and pressed it into her stomach.

Tiffany sat next to her and put a hand on her shoulder.

Angelica's phone rang. The display indicated it was her assistant in L.A.

She squared her shoulders. "Hi, Becky. What's up?" It was very early on the West Coast.

"I just got a message from someone at the Cheyenne office."

"Is something wrong? Did the flood get worse overnight?"

There hadn't been any reports of damage yesterday in

the historic section of town. But it had continued raining all night long.

"Nothing like that," Becky put in quickly. "It's Noah. Apparently he's on an early flight to L.A. this morning."

Angelica came to her feet. "What for?"

"I don't know. But it was a very sudden trip. I can't put my finger on it, but something feels off."

"I'm on my way back. Thanks, Becky." She ended the call.

"What's up?" asked Tiffany.

"You better pack. I'm taking the jet home to find out."

"What happened?"

"One of the hostile vice presidents, Noah, is on his way to L.A. It could be nothing. It might be nothing. But I know he's tight with Ken and Louie, and I need to get to them first.

Angelica crossed to the dresser. She put back the blue jeans and T-shirt and moved to the closet instead. There, she selected a white blouse and a pair of black slacks to go with a tailored black blazer.

She felt more like herself again. She knew she'd feel even better once she got back to the L.A. office.

Noah beat Angelica to L.A., and when she arrived at the office, he was already meeting with Ken Black and Louie Huntley, vice presidents of drama and comedy series respectively. She was annoyed by Noah's move, but there was nothing specific to call him on. Vice presidents met with each other all the time, with or without the CEO.

In the newly decorated boardroom, the landscape of Big Blue hanging proudly on the wall, the men were deep in a discussion. As she walked in and made herself known, Noah was just saying that LBS should continue to create all of its own content. What's more, he announced that her father would have wanted it that way.

"Angelica," said Ken in obvious surprise. "You're back,"

"I'm back," said agreed.

"You're all right?" asked Louie.

"I'm fine," said Angelica. She turned to Noah. "You were saying?"

"Welcome back," said Noah, his tone tight.

There was an awkward silence.

"It's a cornerstone of the network." Ken voiced his agreement with Noah, saying to Angelica, "It's how we distinguish ourselves from the competition. Lassiter Media *is* Lassiter programming. It's not up to you or anyone else to change that."

Becky quietly took a seat at the far end of the table.

"You have to admit, the industry is changing," said Angelica. "Take a look at some of the innovative things happening on cable, even online."

Louie stepped in. "Lassiter will *never* stoop to the trash being played online"

A subtle but satisfied smile played on Noah's lips.

"Who said anything about trash?" she asked them all. "What I'm proposing is new versions of top-rated series, most of them family-friendly. And they were created by our new affiliates, now part of the Lassiter Media family."

"They weren't created by Lassiter Media," said Louie. "Can't you see how you compromise the brand by diluting the creative?"

"They're terrific shows. They're popular shows."

"Since when is mass appeal our primary driver?" asked Ken.

It was on the tip of Angelica's tongue to ask since when vice presidents felt so free to disregard the wishes of the CEO. But she kept silent. She needed to co-opt these men, not alienate them.

"The bottom line still counts," said Angelica.

"So does integrity," said Noah.

"I'm asking you to pull together a team. Pick a series.

Do some storyboards. Let's at least see where it goes." She hadn't made it a direct order, but it was close.

The three men glanced at each other. Then Noah looked at the Big Blue landscape. It was clear he wished he could invoke J.D.

Angelica waited.

"Fine," said Noah. "It's a waste of manpower, but we'll put something together."

"Thank you." Angelica gave a sharp nod, and the men rose and left the boardroom.

Becky shuffled some papers at her end of the table. She'd been J.D.'s executive assistant for the past several years. She'd sat silently through the entire exchange.

Now Angelica turned to her. "What do you think?"

Becky seemed flustered by the question. "I don't know anything about programming decisions."

"You knew my father. You watched him interact with Noah, Ken and Louie, and a whole bunch of other managers."

"You're nicer than he was," said Becky. Then she seemed to catch herself. "That is…I mean…"

"It's okay. If I didn't want your unvarnished opinion, I wouldn't have asked for it."

Becky hesitated a moment longer. "They never would have spoken to Mr. Lassiter like that. They would have said yes, sir, no, sir, how high, sir. And that would have been that."

Angelica couldn't help but smile. "My father brought that out in people."

"He was a very smart man."

"He was. Just out of curiosity, which style do you think works better?"

Again Becky waited a moment before answering. "Maybe somewhere in the middle. Someone has to be at the helm, but other people have good ideas too."

Angelica found herself intrigued by Becky's insight. The woman had long been an observer of senior management meetings, and had been privy to J.D.'s thoughts and opinions on a regular basis.

"What do you think of Max Truger?" Angelica asked.

Again, there was a small hesitation. "I like him. He seems well respected. He's always struck me as smart in meetings. And he's polite to the staff. But then he's younger than a lot of the senior management. I think attitudes have changed over the years. There's not as much hierarchy as there was twenty or thirty years ago."

"I agree with you," said Angelica. "Anybody else that strikes you as progressive?"

"Lana Flynn over in marketing. She's only a manager, but she's bright. And Reece Ogden-Neeves in movies. He's not that young, but he's open-minded."

Angelica liked Reece as well. Though he kept mostly to himself, she'd always thought he was one of the company's strongest assets.

After a pause, Becky said, "I'm not sure why you're asking me this."

"Because you've had a ringside seat to the inner workings for years now. But mostly because I think you're progressive and bright."

Becky smiled at the compliment.

"I'm trying to make something work here," Angelica said. "I'm trying to figure out when to push and when to be patient."

Becky nodded her understanding. "I think you should trust your instincts. I mean, if you're still asking for my opinion."

"Feel free to give your opinion anytime you like," said Angelica. "You trust your instincts too. You've been doing this a long time, and you seem to have a good head on your shoulders."

"Thank you."

"Can you get me a meeting with Reece?"

Becky grinned again. "You're the CEO, Ms. Lassiter. He'll drop everything and come right up."

"I suppose that's true," Angelica agreed. "Let's give it a try and see what happens."

Becky reached to pick up the phone on the boardroom table and connected to Reece's office. It took the man less than three minutes to show up.

"Can you excuse us please, Becky?" Angelica asked as Reece entered the room.

"Of course, Ms. Lassiter."

As Becky left, Reece sat down across the table.

"Is there a problem?" he asked, lips pursed.

"I wanted your opinion on something," said Angelica.

"Of course." He gave a sharp, unsmiling nod. "Whatever you need."

"I'm looking into the possibility of remaking some of the popular series out of the new British and Australian affiliates."

"I heard."

"You did?"

"I also hear you've hit some resistance."

"I have. Are you a resistor?"

Reece gave a slight smile. "I don't know enough about the projects to have an opinion one way or the other."

"In general, do you think we're compromising Lassiter Media's principles by commissioning content from outside that's not original?"

"In general, no. In specific, it depends on whether the content will be embraced by our viewers."

"And how do we determine that?"

"Up front? We can't. We have to try it, and see if it flies."

"Simple as that?"

"Simple as that."

She considered him for a moment. "We might lose a lot of money."

"We might make a lot of money."

"We might lose viewers."

"Or gain them." Reece sat back in his chair. "What are you really asking me?"

The astute question took Angelica by surprise. "If I decide to commission remakes, what can I do that would make you comfortable with the decision?"

"If you're comfortable, then I'm comfortable."

"Are you a yes-man, Reece?"

"In public, yes. In private, I'll give you my opinion, as fully and freely as you want. I'll point out all the potholes in the road. If you tell me to go around them, I will. If you tell me to drive over them, I will. If we crash, we crash. But we'll go down giving it our best shot."

She liked the answer. She liked it a lot. "How's the spring lineup coming?"

He opened a leather folder in front of him. "I brought the draft schedule with me. I thought that's what the meeting was about."

Angelic accepted the report, moving on to their day-to-day business. But she couldn't help thinking that if Reece was working in series instead of movies, her life would be a whole lot easier.

Since they'd returned from Cheyenne, Evan had tried to call Angie several times. She hadn't answered, and she hadn't returned a single message.

He knew he should give up. But some kind of perversity had him tracking her down in person tonight.

He tried to tell himself it was to keep up appearances, but he knew it was because he missed her. It was bad enough before Cheyenne. But since she'd slept in his arms, he hadn't been able to get her out of his head for a moment.

As of five o'clock today, he was the proud, one-third

owner of the Sagittarius Resort. He was pumped and excited, and he wanted to share it with her.

He'd gone ahead with the idea of setting up a trust for J.D.'s money. The trust was receiving a guaranteed return from the investment in Sagittarius, as well as having a profit position in the company. Inspired by the Cheyenne flood, he'd chosen disaster relief as the focus of the fund. There were plenty of ordinary families deserving assistance after any number of floods and storms.

Now, the elevator doors slid open on the twenty-eighth floor of the Lassiter Media building. He'd called Angie's office earlier with no success. Then he'd swung by the mansion, hoping she'd be home by nine o'clock. She wasn't, and her housekeeper confirmed that she didn't have a social engagement tonight. The Lassiter Media offices looked like his best hope.

The door to her temporary office was wide open, and she glanced up at the sound of his footsteps.

"What are *you* doing here?" she asked, looking past him. "And how did you get in the building?"

"I have some news. And the security guards all know me. The world thinks we're engaged again, remember?"

"I remember." She sat back in her leather chair.

He moved around the table. "What are you working on so late?"

"Storyboards."

"Reviewing them?"

"Fixing them."

"You're fixing somebody's storyboards?" It was a surprisingly low-level task. "You're the *CEO*, Angie."

"I'm aware of that."

"Why? What?" It was nine o'clock at night, for pity's sake.

"It's one of the series out of Australia."

He peered over her shoulder. "Not to backseat drive on

you, but don't you have staff who can do this? Maybe even
during regular working hours?"

"How is that not backseat driving?"

"You should have gone home a long time ago."

"It's fine."

"Angie," he warned.

"Don't start in on the work-life balance lecture."

"Then tell me what's going on."

"It's Noah. And Ken and Louie for that matter." She
seemed to hesitate. "I'm not so sure my approach is working."

Evan glanced at the panels on her computer screen, but
they were out of context and didn't make sense. "What approach?"

"I basically ordered them to pick a series and work on
a remake."

"Okay." He didn't really see a problem with that. If the
VPs were going to be snarky, they deserved what they got.

"Their hearts just aren't in it."

"Their ideas aren't working?" Evan's suspicions were
immediately aroused.

"Not at all. I'm playing with this one. I'm thinking if I can
show them what I mean, give them an example using one of
the series, things will smooth out on all three."

Evan glanced at this watch. "So you're working half the
night because your VPs can't get their jobs done."

"I'd like to have something for the morning."

"Not a good plan, Angie."

"Truly none of your business, Evan." She rose from her
chair. "You want some coffee?"

"Not this late."

She moved to a side counter and grabbed the coffee pot.

"Have you had dinner?" he asked her, wrinkling his nose
at the stale smell of the coffee.

"I had a late lunch in the café." She sniffed at the coffee
pot. "Right now, I wish it was still open."

"You want to go out for something?"

She shook her head. "I have to get this done."

He could see arguing would get him nowhere, so he changed the subject. "I've tried to call you a few times since we got back."

She poured the remains of the coffee pot into her cup. "I've been busy working."

"Every night?"

"Most nights, yes."

"You know, this is exactly what J.D. worried about."

She made an abrupt turn to face him. "Bully for J.D. and his perfectly balanced life. But he had *me* for support. He had *you* for support. And he had the loyalty of his entire staff. I'm operating under just a few more challenges than my father." Then her shoulders drooped. "Can we not talk about this? I don't have the energy to fight. Tell me why you came. You said you had news."

Evan wanted to keep hammering home his point. He wanted to grab her and shake some sense into her. Then he wanted to kiss her and make love to her. After that, he feared he might actually want to marry her. But the look on her face told him to keep that all to himself.

"We bought the Sagittarius," he told her instead.

She looked impressed. "You actually did it?"

"We'll make the announcement on Monday."

Her body relaxed a bit more, and she gave him a smile. "That's great news, Evan. I'm truly happy for you."

"I'm happy, too. I can't wait to start working with Deke and Lex." The fit between the three men felt perfect. He was more excited about his professional life than he'd been in months, maybe years.

But he was worried about Angie right now. Even when she smiled, her face was pinched. He wondered if her shoulder was still bothering her. Without conscious thought, he moved closer.

"Do you need to find some more help?" he asked. "Because, you're right, you know. Your father had both of us to share the load. Who've you got?"

She broadened her smile. "This is just a hiccup, Evan. It's all going to work itself out."

"I can—"

"No, you can't." Her tone was firm.

His cellphone rang in his pocket. He wanted to continue arguing with her, but she looked so fragile that he honestly couldn't bring himself to cause her any more distress.

He went for the phone instead.

"It's Matt," he told her as he took the call.

"Hey, Matt."

"Hi, Evan. How are things in L.A.?"

"All's well. How about Cheyenne?"

"We're working hard. Everybody's working hard. There's a lot to do here."

"I bet there is."

"The donation from Lassiter Media has been extremely well received."

"You should tell Angie, not me."

"Yeah, I keep forgetting. You might be back in the family, but you're not back in the firm."

"That's right," Evan agreed, watching Angie as he spoke, battling a desire to draw her into his arms and hold her comfortingly close.

"Kayla and I have come up with a new idea for the wedding," said Matt.

"Oh, yeah?"

"We'd like to have it here in Cheyenne. On the weekend."

"This weekend?"

"Yeah, yeah. I know what you're thinking. We must seem pretty impulsive to you. But I promise, you don't have to lift a finger this time."

"It's not that—"

"We'll have a simple ceremony."

"What about Kayla's mother?"

Matt's tone hardened. "She can come to us. Flights go both ways, you know. We're going to have a small wedding in the church, followed by a big bash at the town hall. The entire ranching community is invited. It'll be a break from all the cleanup."

Evan had to admit, it sounded like a very good idea. "I'll absolutely be there. And I'm sure the town will appreciate it."

The curiosity was clear on Angie's face.

"I think they will," said Matt. "So far, everyone's on board. A whole bunch of people are stepping up to help. Kayla's going to call Angie."

"She's right here," said Evan.

Though it didn't really matter anymore, he couldn't help thinking that the two of them being together helped validate their ruse.

"Ask her if she can make it."

Evan covered the phone. "Can you make it to Kayla and Matt's wedding in Cheyenne this weekend?"

Her jaw dropped.

"She'll be there," Evan told Matt.

"That's great," said Matt.

Angie's mouth moved, but no sounds came out.

"We can't wait," said Evan. "See you in a couple of days."

"Thanks, man."

"No problem." Evan ended the call.

"Cheyenne?" Angie asked, apparently regaining the power of speech.

"They've invited the entire ranching community to the reception. I think it's there way of supporting their neighbors."

"It's a lovely thought," said Angie. But her voice was flat as she dropped down into a chair. "I wish I had more time."

"Oh, no you don't. This is important. You'll spend whatever time it takes to make Kayla happy."

Angie gestured to her computer. "And who will take care of all this?"

"Your employees."

"My employees are rebelling."

"Well, that's a whole other problem. But your best friend is getting married, and you are going to be there with bells on."

Ten

Kayla had swapped her satin, jeweled wedding gown for a simpler dress. It was strapless, with a tight bodice covered in flat, ivory lace. The ankle-length skirt was made of raw silk and wispy chiffon, with a ghost pattern of pale lavender flowers. It was set off by a pair of soft, cream leather ankle boots, while a lavender ribbon had been woven into Kayla's light brown braid that dangled down the center of her back. The effect was simple and beautiful.

Angelica and Tiffany wore matching strapless, purple dresses. They had short, layered skirts. Taupe cowboy boots completed the look.

Barbecues smoldered on the deck of the big hall. Guests had feasted on steaks and grilled salmon prepared by the chefs of the local Lassiter Grill. Dessert would be the gorgeous multi-tiered lemon raspberry cake, baked and decorated by Lassiter Grill's head pastry chef.

After the ceremony and celebratory dinner were both over, Angelica's mind bounced between Cheyenne and L.A. She was delighted for Kayla and Matt but worried about the argument she'd had with Ken this morning.

A local band played on the small stage, and the guests had all gathered around the edges of the worn, hardwood floor.

The first waltz played to an end, and strains of another slow country tune came up. It was Angelica and Evan's signal to join the bride and groom on the dance floor.

Dressed in a steel-gray suit and a pair of cowboy boots, Evan took her hand, walking her to the center of the floor, where he took her in his arms. Her feet automatically picked up the rhythm, and she followed his lead, fighting the urge to settle against his chest, close her eyes and forget about the rest of the world.

"Your head's not here," he said to her.

"My head's right here," she countered. "So are my arms, my legs and my feet."

"You're thinking about Lassiter Media."

"You can read my mind now?"

"I can read your expression. And you keep looking at Noah and frowning."

"I've been smiling all day." At least she had been when-ever she wasn't alone. "And I've been looking at Kayla. Isn't she beautiful?"

"You need to set it aside."

"Set aside the fact that the bride is beautiful? You think I'm jealous?"

Evan gave her a spin then reeled her back.

"Forget about work," he told her. "This is a wedding. You're supposed to be having fun."

"I am having fun."

"You're worrying at about a million miles an hour."

She pasted a bright smile on her face. "I'm having a blast."

Just then, she caught sight of Noah. He, Ken and Louie had come to the wedding, along with many of the other Lassiter managers and staff, since Matt had worked with them for many years. The three men were clustered in a cor-ner, talking intensely to one another. While she watched, a woman joined the conversation. It was Noah's secretary, and she handed him a cell phone. Noah broke away, his glance catching Angelica's for a brief second.

Evan tugged her tight against his chest. "Stop it," he rasped in her ear. Then he turned her so she couldn't see.

"They're up to something," she told him.

Evan drew back. "Let it go. Your job can't be twenty-four seven."

"The networks run twenty-four seven."

"That makes it even more important for you to be able to get away. My hotel is open, but I'm not checking texts."

"You're not in a duel with your managers."

The song changed, but they kept right on dancing.

"Is the duel still going on?" asked Evan.

"It is. And that's what I'm worried about." She'd given Ken the updated storyboards, and he'd told her he'd play with them some more. She'd been waiting two days now for an update.

"What happened?"

"I think Ken's messing up my storyboards."

"So, ask him."

"I did. He's ducking the questions."

"Take charge, Angie. But do it on Monday. For now, dance with me."

"I can't—" She stopped herself mid-protest. There was no point in arguing any further with Evan. They'd just go round and round.

She forced herself to relax into his chest. She concentrated on the dance steps, on the feel of his strong arms, the scent of his skin, the sound of his heartbeat. The music filled her ears, and a rush of desire tightened her chest. If only she could escape with Evan, go somewhere for the night, or even an hour, and let their passion obliterate all the worries in her world.

"That's better." His voice rumbled against her ear. "You, me, Cheyenne. For some reason, it always feels right."

She knew she should argue that. His words were far too

loaded and intimate. But he was right. There was something in the untamed atmosphere, or maybe it was the glorious, star-filled nights. But it pushed them together.

"I want you, Angie."

Her throat closed over, and she couldn't speak.

He drew her hand in close and placed a soft kiss on the inside of her wrist. Sensation bloomed along her arm, warming the core of her body.

The song ended, and the master of ceremonies announced the cake cutting. His hearty voice jangled through the speakers, shocking Angelica back to her senses. What was wrong with her?

She pulled away from Evan and hurried off the dance floor. She'd been about to say yes. She'd been about to agree to yet another night in his arms, in his bed. How could she be so foolish?

She made it into the coat room, where it was dim and quiet. There, she grasped a shelf on the wall, steadying herself and taking deep, calming breaths.

"I'd like to see the lowest rated," said a male voice.

Angelica blinked, realizing the man speaking was around the corner from her, out of sight.

"Was that last year?" It was Noah who was talking. "So, season three?"

Angelica started toward him.

"A copy of the script would be perfect. Yes, please."

She came around the corner, and Noah spotted her. He immediately snapped his jaw shut.

"I'll call you back." He ended the call.

"Who was that?" she asked.

"Australia."

"Who in Australia?"

"Her name is Cathy, low-level assistant, nobody you'd know."

"What are you doing, Noah?"

He started to move for the exit. "Just getting some background information for the remake."

"You're working on a remake from Britain."

"Ken's remake."

Her suspicions were growing. "You've seen the storyboards?"

"The updated ones, yes."

"My updates?"

"Plus Ken's. You had some good ideas, Angie. I'll give you that."

"You'll *give* me that? Why, thank you, Noah. Nice of you to believe I have something to contribute to Lassiter Media."

"What's going on here?" Evan interrupted from behind her.

"Of course you have something to contribute," said Noah, his tone smoothing out. "You have plenty to contribute. Isn't that what I just said?"

For a second, she wondered if she could have possibly misinterpreted his meaning.

"We all loved your changes. We've elaborated on them."

"Why are you working on Ken's project?"

"Enough," said Evan. "Noah, this isn't the time or place."

"Butt out," Angelica said to Evan.

"Leave," Evan said to Noah.

Looking nervous, Noah glanced at Angelica. Then his attention shot back to Evan. A flash of trepidation appeared in his eyes, and he suddenly rushed past them for the door.

Angelica turned on Evan, struggling not to shout. "You can't undermine me like that."

His voice was flat. "They're cutting the cake."

"I don't give a damn about the cake."

He stepped forward, nearly pressing up against her. "Do you hear yourself? Do you?"

"He was talking to the affiliate in Australia, asking about

low-rated shows. I think they might actually be out to get me. I couldn't ignore it."

"Yes, you could. You can. You'll deal with this in the office on Monday."

"Is that an order?"

He clamped his jaw tight. "It's a friendly suggestion."

"You lost the right to make friendly suggestions."

"Did your father's machinations mean nothing to you? Did he put me, your brothers, the company, and everyone else through the ringer for six months and have you not learn a *single lesson?*"

"Shut up, Evan."

"No, I won't shut up. I can't shut up. You want to hear an order, Angie? If I was going to give you an order, here's what it would be. Fire Noah. Fire Ken. Fire Louie. Promote Max. Promote anyone you think you can trust. Then back off, Angie. Back off and let them do their jobs. You cannot do it all alone. You'll botch it, and you'll ruin your life."

Angelica's pulse pounded in anger. She'd been around Lassiter Media a whole lot longer than Evan. *She* was the one her father trusted. *She* was the one in charge. She all but growled at him. "Are you actually telling me how to run my company?"

"No," Evan answered softly. Then he lifted her left hand, rubbing his thumb across the diamond in her ring. "I'm telling you how to be my wife."

The world stopped dead in its tracks.

"A long time ago," he continued, "I met a beautiful, cheerful, wonderful woman. I fell in love with her, and I wanted to spend the rest of my life keeping her happy. But you've taken her, Angie. You've stolen her from me and I can't seem to get her back."

He let go of her hand, and his voice flattened out. "If she ever shows up again, give me a call." Then he turned and walked away.

Angelica started to shake. She gripped a shelf again, feeling woozy. She hadn't gone anywhere. She was still here. If Evan loved her, if he'd truly loved her, he'd know that she was all one package. He wasn't allowed to pull her apart, discarding anything that was less than perfect. That wasn't how love worked.

Evan spent three days regretting his outburst. Back in L.A., it played through his head over and over again. He'd pushed too hard. He'd pushed too fast. She might someday be ready to put her life on an even keel, but she wasn't there yet. He should have given her more time.

"Premier Tech Corporation conferences," Lex announced triumphantly as he walked into Evan's office at Sagittarius. "Five-year commitment, five days each month as they rotate through their regions, five hundred guests per conference."

"This came out of Deke's contact?" asked Evan, shifting his mind to business.

"On the strength of the commitment, we're sending you to trade shows in Munich, London and Paris." Lex slapped a stack of conference brochures down on Evan's desk. "Corporate business is the most lucrative of all. You leave Friday. Pick five staff to take along."

"I don't get a say in my own schedule?" Evan lifted an itinerary from the top of the stack.

"You're overseas expansion. Besides, it's London and Paris, not Siberia. Who doesn't love going to London and Paris?"

"I suppose," said Evan.

It was a great opportunity. And he knew he was foolish to keep waiting on Angie. She was stuck in her world, and he was quickly moving into his own. It couldn't be clearer that she didn't want his advice, that she didn't want him.

He leafed through a conference brochure from the stack. "I suppose I should start building a marketing team."

Lex sat down. "You can hire new, or you can see if we have any likely candidates already on staff."

"I like Gabrielle down in client relations. She's originally from Paris. She's fluent in French and Italian."

"She's also smokin' hot."

Evan frowned. "Now that's a quick route to a sexual harassment lawsuit."

Not that he was interested in any woman at the moment. If it wasn't Angie, well, he was going to have to take some time to think about how that worked.

"What I meant was, she might have some hot friends back home."

"I'll keep that in mind," said Evan.

"So Angie broke it off with you?"

Evan was through pretending. "We haven't spoken since the wedding."

"Isn't that pretty much the same thing?"

"I guess." Except that they'd never actually gotten back together in the first place. "It was doomed from the start."

"You okay?" asked Lex.

"I'll be fine. It's not like I haven't had six months to get used to the idea."

Lex considered him for a moment. "I get the feeling you never did. And having her back, well…you two seemed good together, Evan."

"We were, until we weren't anymore."

"Can the good times come back?"

"I thought maybe. For a while at least, I'd hoped so." The image of her sleeping in his arms at Big Blue surfaced in his mind. "For a little while there, I really thought we had another chance."

"Maybe you'll get over her in Paris."

"Maybe."

Lex came to his feet. "Take Gabrielle along. Hopefully her friends can help out."

Evan managed a smile. But a fling in France wasn't in the cards. He couldn't imagine making love to anyone but Angie.

Mid-morning, Angelica stared across the boardroom table at Noah and Ken. She'd wanted to be right. She'd desperately wanted to be right and for Evan to be wrong. The last thing her self-esteem needed was for her ex-fiancé to be better than she was at running her family's company.

"These are terrible," she said to the two men, covering the screen of her tablet computer on the revised storyboards.

Noah jumped in. "We think they're very much in keeping with the overall—"

"No," said Angelica. "They're terrible. And, what's more, you both know it." Her anger was rapidly replacing her disappointment. "You want this project to fail. You don't agree with the direction I'm taking, and you want to prove your point by compromising the project."

This time, Ken tried. "We took what you said and—"

"No," Angelica repeated. "You deliberately undermined me. And you compromised the good of Lassiter Media to support your own agenda. You don't get to do that."

She rose to her feet. Then she hit a speed dial button on her cell phone. Her assistant immediately answered.

"Becky? Please send security in here right away."

The color drained from Noah's and Ken's faces.

"Are you all right?" Becky asked.

"I'm fine."

There was a briefest of pauses. "They'll be right in."

Angelica set down her phone. "Someone from the finance department will be in touch with a severance package. It will include your pension plans. For now, security will escort you to your offices so you can pick up your personal belongings."

The boardroom door opened, and two Lassiter security guards entered the room.

"These two gentlemen are leaving Lassiter Media's employ immediately," Angelica said to the security guards. "Please give them a chance to pick up any personal items. They'll need to leave their company cell phones and their keys. And have the IT department shut down their accounts. I'll make arrangements with the Cheyenne office."

Noah came to his feet, and the two security guards instantly moved toward him.

"You can't fire us," he shouted.

Ken rose as well, but he seemed more stunned than angry.

"I just did," said Angelica, gathering her things.

"We have the support of the creative team!" Noah shouted.

"And I'm the CEO." She headed for the door.

"You'll *regret this*." Noah's voice followed her out.

Becky was there to meet her. "Are you okay?" She took the tablet from Angelica's hands.

"I'm fine. Really fine." A weight felt like it had been literally lifted from Angelica's shoulders.

"Can I get you anything?" asked Becky, her glance going furtively over her shoulder to where security was escorting Noah and Ken the opposite direction down the hallway.

"I'm heading down to twenty-one. Can you free up my next two hours?"

"Absolutely."

"Thank you." Angelica pushed the button for the elevator.

She made her way to the twenty-first floor, to Reece Ogden-Neeves's office.

"Angelica?" He looked surprised, but quickly asked the man and woman in his office to excuse them.

"I'm sorry to barge in," she began as he closed the door behind them.

"Not at all." He motioned to a chair at the meeting table next to his picture window.

Angelica couldn't help but note that L.A. was moving along as normal. Traffic was brisk. The flags were blowing.

And clouds were moving in from the ocean. It was going to be another beautiful afternoon.

She sat down, and Reece took the chair opposite.

"I've just fired Noah and Ken," she told him without preamble.

The surprise was clear on Reece's face.

"Louie is next."

"I see."

"I've decided to create two senior vice president positions, one for core operations and one for new ventures and expansion. My initial thought was you for core operations and Max Truger for expansion."

"So, you're not firing me?"

Angelica cracked a smile. "No, I'm not firing you."

"I wasn't sure there for a moment."

"Did I bury the lead?"

He grinned. "You did. And Max Truger?"

"What do you think?"

"I think he's great. He's smart, innovative and fearless."

"Is fearless bad or good?"

"Depends on your tolerance for risk."

"High," she answered.

Today it was very high. She was taking risks at Lassiter Media, starting now. But she was about to take an even bigger, personal risk right afterward.

"Then Max is your guy."

"I need people I can trust," she told Reece. "People who see the future the way I see it, and in whom I can put a lot of faith and decision-making power. This isn't a one-woman operation."

"It's not," Reece agreed.

"Are you up for the challenge?"

"I am."

Angelica rose, and Reece stood with her.

"I'm going to fire Louie now," she said. "After that, you want to come to Cheyenne and help me promote Max?"

Reece reached out to shake her hand, his smile going wide. "I'd like nothing better."

"The car will be out front in half an hour. It'll be a whirlwind trip. I have something I need to do in L.A. tonight."

Evan was in no rush to get home. His flight left for Frankfurt at nine in the morning, and he didn't feel like facing an empty apartment tonight. Instead, he levered himself into a high leather seat in the Sagittarius sports bar. The chair was comfortable. The brickwork detail and low lighting gave a pleasing ambiance. And a major league game was just getting underway on the big screen.

He ordered a beer from the bartender. Barry was the man's name, and Evan had spoken with him a few times over the past week. But tonight, Evan didn't want to chat. He wanted to think. He wanted to sort through his emotions fully and finally, and leave it all behind when he got on the plane.

Maybe he would have a fling in Paris. Why not? Celibacy wasn't a realistic long-term strategy. He might as well get started now. Get that first encounter under his belt, and maybe it would become easier with time.

"This seat taken?" The soft voice sent a shot of reaction up his spine.

He turned slowly to see Angie standing beside him. She looked gorgeous and uncertain. Her hair was half up, half down, softly curled. She was wearing a pale pink dress with spaghetti straps and a layered skirt.

"Can I get you a drink?" asked the bartender.

"Brandonville Chablis," Evan quickly answered for her, hoping she'd feel obligated to stay for a while.

She climbed up onto the seat. "I was on my way home from work."

"Dressed like that?"

"I changed before I left the office." She set a small purse down on the bar. "I…uh…well. I wanted to give you something."

She reached out her hand, opening her fist.

He looked down and saw the circle of his engagement ring sitting in her palm. His heart froze, sending a sharp pain through the middle of his chest.

He'd known it would hurt. But he hadn't expected to feel like he was drowning. For a split second, he wondered if he'd ever breathe again.

"Charade's over?" he managed.

"Charade's over."

When he didn't take the ring, she set it on the bar in front of them. He couldn't bring himself to look at it.

"I fired Noah today," she told him conversationally.

The bartender set down the glass of Chablis. He glanced at Evan, looking like he might join in the conversation. But Evan's expression obviously warned him off, and he moved briskly away.

"Probably a good call," Evan told her.

"Then I fired Ken."

That got Evan's attention.

"Well," she continued. "I actually fired them both at the same time."

"What happened?"

She toyed with the stem of her wineglass. "You were right, and I was wrong."

He gave his head a little shake. "Excuse me?"

She looked at him. "Are you going to make me say it again? Because it's embarrassing. It seems you can run Lassiter Media better than me."

He struggled to wrap his head around her words. "What *happened*?"

"They were sabotaging me."

He paused. "Somehow, that doesn't come as a complete shock."

"I mean, it's one thing to disagree with your boss. And it's one thing to press your point. But to try to make something fail? To waste the company's resources? No. That wasn't going to happen. I fired Louie too." She lifted the glass to her lips.

"He was in on it?" Evan asked.

"Thick as thieves. I've never done anything like that before." She took another drink. "I need this."

Evan resisted an urge to take her hand. "I'm proud of you, Angie."

"Thank you. I'm a little proud of myself."

"You should be." His glance went to the diamond ring on the polished bar top.

"I promoted Reece."

"Reece is a good man."

Evan realized that Angie had finally come to her senses. The woman he loved was back, but she was breaking up with him all over again. The pain in his chest radiated out.

"We went to Cheyenne together."

"You and Reece?"

She nodded, and Evan felt a stab of jealousy.

He reached out and picked up the ring. That was it, then. It was over. He dropped the ring into his shirt pocket. He was going to have to stay away from Reece Ogden-Neeves for a while. Otherwise, he might end up with an assault charge on his record.

"I wanted Reece to be there when I promoted Max Truger. I'm really going to count on the two of them."

"You promoted Max?" Evan couldn't help but be pleased about that.

Angie turned and looked him in the eyes; hers were soft and fathomlessly dark. "You were right, and I was wrong. I need help at the top. I need it from people I can trust. And then I need to back off and let them do their jobs, so I can have a life."

He loved her. He loved her so much it hurt.

His throat was raw. "But you're giving me back the ring?"

"The engagement was fake, Evan."

He knew that. But it didn't change how he felt.

"I don't want a fake engagement." Her gaze fixed on his shirt pocket. "If I'm going to wear that ring again, it has to be real."

It took a moment for her words to penetrate. When they did, he couldn't believe it. "Are you saying…?"

She nodded.

He came to his feet, his body all but vibrating with joy. But this couldn't happen here. It couldn't happen in a sports bar.

He drew her from her chair, then out of the bar, down the wide hallway. It took him a moment to figure out where to go. But then he used his access key to let them into the dim, closed spa. He pushed the door shut, locking it behind them.

"Marry me," he told her, wrapping her in his arms. "Marry me, marry me, marry me."

"Yes," she answered simply, her dark eyes shimmering.

He kissed her then, deeply, thoroughly, passionately.

"I love you, Angie."

"I love you, Evan. I never thought I'd get to say that again."

He scooped her into his arms. "Say it as much as you like. Say it every day." He started to walk.

"Where are we going?"

"I don't know." He made his way down a narrow hallway. "I've never been in here. But I'm betting there's something back here that resembles a bed."

"We're going to make love in the spa?"

"It's closed and locked, and I own the place. So, yes, we're going to make love in the spa." They came into a lounge area with a softly lit fountain. He spotted a wide, low sofa.

"Here we go." He set her down on the sofa and gazed at the picture she made. "I love you in pink. You should always wear pink. Now, take it off."

She grinned up at him. "I just fired three men for not being deferential."

"Oh, I'll be deferential. I'll be *very* deferential. Just as soon as you're naked."

She held out her hand, wiggling her fingers. "Can I have my ring first?"

He dropped down on one knee, pulling the ring from his pocket. Then he smoothly pushed it onto her left hand. "This is *never* coming off."

"This is," she lightly joked. She slipped her fingers from his hand, drew back and pulled the dress over her head, tossing it to one side.

Epilogue

Spring had arrived at Big Blue. Flowers were blooming, birds chirping, and the bright sunshine heated the lush hills. Evan had warned Angie they were taking a chance with the garden wedding, but now he was glad they'd risked it. The sky was a perfect, vast blue. White folding chairs were set up on the lawn, azaleas, peonies and tulips making the landscape colorful.

Angie had walked alone down the aisle toward Evan and the preacher, who were standing under the natural wood canopy. Her brothers and Chance had all offered to escort her, but she'd said J.D. was with her, his presence in everything about Big Blue.

Evan had never seen her looking more beautiful. She'd chosen a simple white dress, knee length, made of delicate chiffon. Crisscrossing to a low, V back, the spaghetti straps left her shoulders bare. She'd woven wildflowers in her upswept hair and carried a tiny, cornflower bouquet.

It was nothing like he'd originally imagined their wedding, but it was perfect. And when he'd kissed his bride, he knew they were ready to stand together through anything life might throw at them.

Much later, he stood with Chance at the edge of a garden overlooking the natural swimming pool. The stars were a sparkling canopy above the ranch, while tiny, white lights decorated a temporary dance floor. Angie was dancing with her brother Dylan, while his wife Jenna watched, holding their baby son.

Deke was dancing with a dazzling Tiffany. Evan was in on the secret that his friend was proposing to her tomorrow night.

"Have you picked out a spot yet?" asked Chance, smiling, his gaze resting on his wife Felicia as she stopped to talk to Jenna. Felicia was several months pregnant with what they had just discovered were twins.

"Angie says we should build in the meadow beside Rustle Creek." Evan couldn't help but smile at the memory of their conversation. "I say a hundred feet up the hillside in case there's ever another flood."

Chance chuckled. "Don't blame you for that."

Although the ranchers had completely recovered from the fall flooding, nobody wanted to go through anything like that again.

"I can deed you the property," said Chance. "As much of it as you'd like."

Evan shook his head. "Not necessary. I don't think Angie wants to break the place up into pieces."

"She's keeping the mansion in L.A.?"

"She's not interested in letting go of any of the family possessions. We'll be here part-time, but we'll still need roots in L.A."

"It's a big house for two people." Chance gave Evan a sidelong glance.

"We hope it won't just be the two of us for long." Evan and Angie had tossed out her birth control pills last month. They were both content to let the babies come along whenever it happened.

Chance's gaze went back to Felicia and Jenna. "It looks like the Lassiter clan will be growing in leaps and bounds."

"I'm more than willing to do my part."

"I've set the bar pretty high," said Chance.

Evan laughed at the reference to the twins. He gazed around at the crowds of happy people, including Marlene dancing with the senior partner from Logan's law firm. The two had been inseparable since Christmas. Sage and his wife Colleen had announced they were also expecting a baby.

"I can't help but think J.D. would be happy with all this," he told Chance.

"I can guarantee he would," said Chance. "He'd have loved all the grandchildren, and especially the strong bonds between the family members."

Evan nodded his understanding and agreement.

The band ended the lively song then slowed things down to a waltz. Angie glanced around, and Evan knew it was his cue to join her.

"Catch you later," he told Chance, his feet taking him toward his bride.

"Later," Chance answered from behind him.

Angelica caught sight of Evan and flashed him a brilliant smile. His heart warmed, and the world around him seemed to disappear. He quickened his pace, scooping her into his arms, drawing her tight as they settled into the slow rhythm of the music.

"Hello, Mrs. McCain," he intoned next to her ear.

"Hello, Mr. McCain." She molded against him, letting him support her slight weight.

"Are you getting tired?"

"A little bit. But it's been a fantastic day, don't you think? Everyone seems really happy."

"As long as you're happy," he said. "That's all that counts."

"I am happy, Evan. I'm incredibly happy."

"I told Chance we wanted to build in the meadow."

She drew her head back. "Is he okay with that?"

"He's fine with it. I think he's looking forward to all the little Lassiter grandchildren that'll soon be running around Big Blue. He's bragging about his significant contribution to the effort."

"Felicia's the one doing all the work."

"He's still taking credit."

Angie went silent for a few minutes, swaying to the music.

"We can say goodnight anytime you want," he told her.

Chance had a horse-drawn carriage waiting to take them in true Big Blue style to a little cottage in the hills for their wedding night.

"A few more minutes," said Angie.

"Sure."

She drew a deep sigh. "It feels like the Lassiters are start-ing a whole new chapter."

"They are," Evan agreed. "And I am thrilled and proud to be part of it."

"Something fantastic is starting." She gazed up at him, her eyes shimmering in the tiny lights. "But something fantastic is ending too. I just need a little longer to savor the goodbye."

He wrapped her tight in his arms again, with the huge sky above them, the ranch around them, and the joy and good-will of their family permeating the Wyoming night. "Take all the time you need, sweetheart. Take all the time you need."

* * * * *

Dynasties: The Lassiters
Don't miss a single story!

COMING NEXT MONTH FROM

HARLEQUIN

Desire

TM

Available October 7, 2014

#2329 STRANDED WITH THE RANCHER
Texas Cattleman's Club: After the Storm • by Janice Maynard
Feuding neighbors Beth and Drew must take shelter from a devastating
tornado. Trapped by the wreckage, they give in to an attraction that's been
simmering for months. Can they find common ground after the storm settles?

#2330 THE CHILD THEY DIDN'T EXPECT
Billionaires and Babies • by Yvonne Lindsay
After one amazing night, Alison is shocked to learn her lover is her new
client—and he's assumed guardianship of his orphaned nephew. Soon,
she wants this family as her own—but can she stay once she learns the
truth about the baby?

#2331 FOR HER SON'S SAKE
Baby Business • by Katherine Garbera
Driven by family rivalry, Kell takes over single mom Emma's company.
But carrying out his plan means another son will grow up seeking revenge.
Is Kell brave enough to fight *for* Emma, instead of against her, and change
his legacy?

#2332 HER SECRET HUSBAND
Secrets of Eden • by Andrea Laurence
When Julianne and Heath come home to help their family, they're forced
to face their past, including their secret nuptials. As passion brings them
together a second time, will a hidden truth ruin their chance at happiness
again?

#2333 TEMPTED BY A COWBOY
The Beaumont Heirs • by Sarah M. Anderson
Rebellious cowboy Phillip Beaumont meets his match in horse trainer
Jo Spears. He's never had to chase a woman, but the quiet beauty won't
let him close—which only makes him more determined to tempt her into
his bed....

#2334 A HIGH STAKES SEDUCTION • by Jennifer Lewis
While the straight-laced Constance investigates the books at
John Fairweather's casino, she's secretly thrilled by the mysterious
owner's seduction. But the numbers don't lie. Can she trust the longing
in his eyes, or is he playing another game?

HDCNM0914

REQUEST YOUR FREE BOOKS!

2 FREE NOVELS PLUS 2 FREE GIFTS!

HARLEQUIN® *Desire*

ALWAYS POWERFUL, PASSIONATE AND PROVOCATIVE

YES! Please send me 2 FREE Harlequin Desire® novels and my 2 FREE gifts (gifts are worth about $10). After receiving them, if I don't wish to receive any more books, I can return the shipping statement marked "cancel." If I don't cancel, I will receive 6 brand-new novels every month and be billed just $4.55 per book in the U.S. or $4.99 per book in Canada. That's a savings of at least 13% off the cover price! It's quite a bargain! Shipping and handling is just 50¢ per book in the U.S. and 75¢ per book in Canada.* I understand that accepting the 2 free books and gifts places me under no obligation to buy anything. I can always return a shipment and cancel at any time. Even if I never buy another book, the two free books and gifts are mine to keep forever.

225/326 HDN F4ZC

Name _____ (PLEASE PRINT) _____

Address _____ Apt. # _____

City _____ State/Prov. _____ Zip/Postal Code _____

Signature (if under 18, a parent or guardian must sign) _____

Mail to the **Harlequin® Reader Service:**

IN U.S.A.: P.O. Box 1867, Buffalo, NY 14240-1867
IN CANADA: P.O. Box 609, Fort Erie, Ontario L2A 5X3

Want to try two free books from another line?
Call 1-800-873-8635 or visit www.ReaderService.com.

* Terms and prices subject to change without notice. Prices do not include applicable taxes. Sales tax applicable in N.Y. Canadian residents will be charged applicable taxes. Offer not valid in Quebec. This offer is limited to one order per household. Not valid for current subscribers to Harlequin Desire books. All orders subject to credit approval. Credit or debit balances in a customer's account(s) may be offset by any other outstanding balance owed by or to the customer. Please allow 4 to 6 weeks for delivery. Offer available while quantities last.

Your Privacy—The Harlequin® Reader Service is committed to protecting your privacy. Our Privacy Policy is available online at www.ReaderService.com or upon request from the Harlequin Reader Service.

We make a portion of our mailing list available to reputable third parties that offer products we believe may interest you. If you prefer that we not exchange your name with third parties, or if you wish to clarify or modify your communication preferences, please visit us at www.ReaderService.com/consumerchoice or write to us at Harlequin Reader Service Preference Service, P.O. Box 9062, Buffalo, NY 14269. Include your complete name and address.

HD13R